LITTLE SISTER

"I've been watching you in study hall lately. You concentrate so hard on your homework that nothing seems to distract you. That's why I kicked you. I had to make sure you were really alive."

"You mean you kicked me on purpose?" I pretended to be mad, but of course I was ecstatic.

Ron glanced over at me and chuckled. "Actually, I was getting tired of looking at the back of your head. The front view is a lot better."

"Why, thank you," I said sarcastically, trying to cover my disbelief. The idea that Ron Peters had kicked me on *purpose* really threw me. Ron was a bigshot at school, tall, dark and very popular. He could have any girl he wanted. So what did he want with *me?*

Bantam Sweet Dreams Romances
Ask your bookseller for the books you have missed

Little Sister

Yvonne Greene

BANTAM BOOKS
Toronto · New York · London · Sydney

RL 5, IL age 11 and up

LITTLE SISTER

A Bantam Book / September 1981

2nd printing . . . August 1981	7th printing . . . May 1982
3rd printing . . . October 1981	8th printing . . . August 1982
4th printing . . . December 1981	9th printing . . . September 1982
5th printing . . . January 1982	10th printing . . . November 1982
6th printing . . . March 1982	11th printing . . . September 1983
12th printing . . . December 1983	

Cover photo by Ariel Skelley

ISBN 0-553-24319-5

Published simultaneously in the United States and Canada

*Bantam Books are published by Bantam Books, Inc. Its trademark,
consisting of the words ''Bantam Books'' and the portrayal of a
rooster, is Registered in U.S. Patent and Trademark Office and in
other countries. Marca Registrada. Bantam Books, Inc., 666 Fifth
Avenue, New York, New York 10103.*

PRINTED IN THE UNITED STATES OF AMERICA

O   21   20   19   18   17   16   15   14   13   12

Little Sister

Chapter One

I woke up on that dark November morning full of gloom. Not the best way to greet your birthday, I thought, glancing at the clock on my night table. 6:34 A.M. In twelve minutes I would be exactly sixteen years old.

Most girls looked forward to turning sixteen. In fact, I used to dream about it. I'd have fantasies of throwing a huge party and inviting the whole junior class. Of course, everyone would come. It would be a night to remember, with music all through the house, Mom's special canapés, and crowds of kids having a great time. My attention, however, would be reserved for the handsomest boy in the room, who would just happen to be my boyfriend.

But I'd learned a long time ago that my dreams

had little relationship to reality. My reality was awful. There was no way I could escape the fact that I, Cindy Halley, would never have a sixteenth birthday that would come close to being as sweet as my sister Christine's.

As if I needed to be reminded why I was so down, my eyes fell on the framed photograph that sat on my night table. It was a picture of me and Christine taken when I was twelve and she was thirteen. Goodness knows why I still kept it next to my bed. Maybe I wanted to remind myself of the one year when Christine and I really acted like sisters. The year when we laughed at each other's jokes and told each other our secret dreams. But the picture of the two of us laughing together was ancient history, something that would never happen again. Because as soon as Christine entered high school she began to act as if I didn't exist. All of a sudden she turned into a beautiful, popular teenager, one of the most sought-after girls in Northdale High School. And I was a nobody. Her little sister.

In fact, I thought, her sixteenth birthday party had been the social event last year. Anybody who was anybody had been invited. Alan Ashley, her boyfriend at the time, had come with his rock band, and he sang every song for Christine. It was so romantic—his eyes never left her face. All in all it had been a perfect June evening. Crowds of kids had partied on the back patio late into the night—long after I had gone up to my room and climbed into bed.

Sighing, I sat up to turn my alarm off. It would be useless, I thought, to have a big party like Christine's. Those kinds of parties were only for girls like her—popular girls who had boyfriends and went out every Saturday night. They weren't for girls like me, who were ugly and had never even been asked out on a date.

That dreadful fact stirred up an uneasy feeling in the pit of my stomach. I'm sixteen today, I thought, and I've never had a boyfriend! Suddenly I felt awful. I lay down and pulled the comforter over my face. Maybe I could convince Mom I was sick and spend the entire day in bed. The thought was appealing.

Just then I heard a knock, and my mother's smiling face appeared from behind the bedroom door. "Happy Birthday to you . . ." she sang, "Happy Birthday to you . . . Happy Birthday, dear Cindy . . . Happy Birthday to you!"

Despite my mood, I couldn't help smiling at her corny, off-key efforts. Then she came into the room carrying a tray. On it were French toast and sausage, fresh-squeezed orange juice, cocoa, and a bud vase with a daisy in it.

"Oh, Mom, you shouldn't have," I said. "You must've gotten up at six to do this."

She bent down and kissed me on the forehead. "It's my pleasure, sweetheart. After all, it's the least I can do. It's your birthday, and you're not even having a par—" She stopped suddenly, leaving the words dangling in mid-air.

I knew what she was about to say. "Oh, Mom," I answered quickly, avoiding her eyes, "I told you I don't want a party. So just forget it. Okay?" Mom had loved helping Christine with her party and she was really disappointed when I said I didn't want one.

The faint laugh lines around my mother's mouth disappeared as her smile faded. I quickly picked up a fork and took a big bite of the hot, sweet French toast. "Umm, good!" I said, smacking my lips and holding out a big piece for my mother to try. "It's delicious!"

She sighed and settled herself comfortably on the edge of my bed. "Well, Cindy," she asked, "how does it feel to be sweet sixteen?"

The words "sweet sixteen" made me feel even worse. "Would you please stop saying 'sweet sixteen'?" I demanded grumpily. "It sounds so old-fashioned, for Pete's sake. Anyway, I'd like to know what's so 'sweet' about it?"

"Oh! I see!" Mom's face registered understanding. You could ask her the most complicated or the most simple question, and she'd always answer, "Oh, I see!"

"Oh, I see *what?*" I asked, annoyed.

"Oh, I see you're a pretty unhappy birthday girl." Mom's voice softened. Even though I was crazy about my mother, I wished she would go away. She had an unpleasant habit of digging down so deep into the heart of a subject that it hurt.

"Oh, no!" I lied, putting another piece of toast into my mouth. "I'm happy. Honest."

"Cindy! There's no need to play games with me. I'm your mother and—"

"And I'm your daughter," I burst out. "But you wouldn't know it, not from the way I look."

"What on earth are you talking about, Cindy?" she asked, surprised.

I looked down and moved a piece of toast around on my plate. "You know what I mean."

"No, I don't." Mom lifted my chin up with her hand and looked straight at me. "Tell me what's the matter."

I tried to stay calm. "You know I don't look a bit like you or Dad," I said. "And especially not like Christine. How do you think it feels, being the ugliest person in the family?"

Mom was struck dumb for a minute. "That's the most ridiculous thing I've ever heard, Cindy," she said. "And you know Dad and I love you and Christine exactly the same."

"I'm not talking about love, Mom," I nearly shouted. "I'm talking about *looks*. You and Dad are both handsome, but I'm just a nothing in the looks department. And if that's not bad enough, my own sister happens to be the most beautiful girl in town..."

Even as I spoke them, the words sounded familiar. They reminded me of my complaints as a child, when I used to say things like: "It's not fair, Mommy. Christine got a bigger piece of cake than I did..." Great, I thought, I'm sixteen and I'm acting like a three-year-old.

I also had a vague sense of having hurt my mother's feelings. Suddenly ashamed, I pushed the breakfast tray aside and said, "Look, Mom, I have to get dressed. I'm sorry...I...thanks for breakfast."

But she continued to stare at me, making no effort to get up. Her eyes looked just as bright and blue as Christine's, only kinder, and with a lot less makeup around them. Although her light hair had darkened a bit, it was still beautiful, framing her face in soft, layered waves.

"You know, Cindy, you let your imagination get the better of you sometimes," she said. "There's nothing at all wrong with your looks."

Immediately I thought of an expression I'd heard often: "The kind of face only a mother could love." It only made me feel worse to think that my own mother was blind to the way I really looked.

"Maybe you don't think there's anything wrong with my looks!" I bit my lips to keep from bursting into tears. "But there's nothing right with them either. Don't you realize I'm sixteen and I've never had a single date with a boy?"

"So *that's* why you didn't want a party." My mother stood up and looked at me knowingly. "You could have asked your friends to bring their boyfriends, couldn't you?" she asked.

I got out of bed and pretended to look around for my clothes. "Oh, super idea! Then I'd be the only girl without a date *at my own party!*" Pulling on a pair of knee socks, I looked up at my mother suspiciously. "Or were you thinking of inviting creepy Richie over to pose as my escort?" "Creepie Richie" was what I called my cousin from Michigan. Not only was he six months younger than I was, but he was several inches shorter, very pimply, and *boring.*

Now Mom was the one who was annoyed. "Cynthia! How can you call your cousin a name like that!"

"Oh, Mom," I wailed. "You have no idea how I feel. You were never ugly."

"And neither are you," she said vehemently. "You happen to be an attractive young woman, just as pretty as Christine, only in a completely different way. And I don't say that just because I'm your mother." Bending over my bed, she picked up the tray. Then, thinking better of it, she sat back down on my bed, balancing the tray on her lap.

Turning away, I started dressing, pulling my brown corduroy pants on under my nightgown. I liked the way the loose, wide-ribbed fabric neatly camouflaged my skinny hips.

"Did you hear me, Cindy?" My mother was still talking to me.

"What did you say, Mom?" I wanted her to go away and leave me alone in my misery.

"I said, remember a couple of years ago when Christine reached the height she is now, and you were upset because you were still short?"

"Yeah, so?" I asked, puzzled.

"Well, look at you now. You're even taller than she is," she answered triumphantly.

"What about it? I *hate* being taller than she is!"

"Nonsense!" my mother said. "It's an asset to be tall, Cindy. You'll see. But what I'm trying to say is, look how you caught up with her. It just took you a little longer, that's all."

"Oh, I see what you're saying, Mom." I pulled a belt on. "It's the old just-wait-and-see stuff. But you can't convince me that it'll be the same with boys."

"Well, we'll see." My mother smiled. "Now I'm not going to leave this room until I see my birthday girl smile."

I turned and gave her the biggest, phoniest smile I could manage. "How's that?" I teased.

"Needs work," Mom laughed as she walked to the door with the tray. "Happy birthday, dear."

Chapter Two

After Mom left, I glanced at myself in the full-length mirror. Yes, it was true what my mother said about my height—I had outgrown Christine by more than two and a half inches. But what good had that done? Now I was taller and lankier than ever, without a single curve in sight. Christine may have been shorter, but she was also a lot curvier—and a lot sexier. Boys seemed to appreciate her height a lot more than they did mine.

Turning to my dresser, I grabbed a brush and ran it through my reddish blonde, shoulder-length hair. Though it was my best asset, it was certainly nothing special. I thought of the thick long, wavy, naturally light-blonde hair that made Christine stand out in any crowd. She'd inherited that from my mother, along with her vibrant blue eyes. I got nothing—even my eyes were a plain, dull brown. I frowned at my image in the mirror. "You're ugly! Ugly!" I snapped.

Pulling my nightgown over my head, I checked out my body. Progress was slow but I did seem to be filling out somewhat. With luck, by the time I got to be Mom's age, I'd have something resembling breasts, I told myself sarcastically. Slipping into a padded bra, I thought about which top to wear. Finally I decided on a sweater with a large cowl neck. It was bright yellow. Maybe the color would pick me up and put me in a better mood.

If it doesn't, I'd still have my dreams, I reassured myself. I'd always been something of a daydreamer, and more than once a teacher had yelled at me for not paying attention in class. But was it my fault that my dream world was so much more exciting than real life?

Just maybe, I thought, I'd meet a boy today, the way girls did in fairy tales. After all, a girl's sixteenth birthday was supposed to be a magical time. Naturally, my dream boy would be tall, good-looking, considerate, and fun to be with. Of course, I didn't believe I'd really meet him today—but I could pretend for now.

I pulled on my sweater and combed out my baby-fine hair. It was too long, I decided. Maybe I should get it cut again. But I'd heard that long hair was popular now with fashion models.

Striking a pose in the mirror, I smiled at myself. Modeling would be a super job, I thought—wearing great clothes all day, and getting your hair and makeup done by real professionals!

Then I remembered a conversation my family had had at dinner only a few nights before.

There we were, Mom and Dad and my sister and I, all happily eating away, when Christine said, very matter-of-factly, "Oh, guess what?" Whenever she says "Oh" in that casual fashion of hers, I just know she's going to tell one of her incredible stories. Christine's in the drama club, and she loves to practice her acting on the rest of us. My mother falls for it every time. That night was no exception.

"What, sweetheart?" she'd asked Christine expectantly.

My sister had shaken her blonde hair off her shoulders with a quick toss of the head and announced. "I'm going to be a model!"

"You're kidding!" Mom had exclaimed, her fork resting in mid-air.

"Nope." Christine looked very pleased with herself. "I'm starting in June."

Mom had acted as if she just couldn't believe it. "But, honey, how did this come about? What about acting?"

"Oh, Mom, of *course* I'm still going to be an actress. But modeling can be a good stepping-stone. Besides, I'll make loads of money!"

"Hold on there a moment!" That was my

father, ever practical. "Would you mind telling us how you got this job? I hope it wasn't from some ad in the paper."

"Oh, no, *of course not!*" Christine had pretended to look shocked, widening her mascara'd eyes. "It happened in school. They have this program called Career Day. It's for kids who aren't planning to attend college next year—"

"But you are," my mother cut in.

"I know," Christine'd answered. "But I can do *both*. Now listen... This woman from the Talent Model Agency in Chicago, Ms. Newson or something, came in to talk about modeling careers, so naturally I went to hear her."

Naturally, I'd thought sarcastically.

Christine went on, "... and after she spoke, she asked everyone who was interested in modeling to see her. So I went up to speak to her and she gave me her address and suggested I come in and see the agency *as soon* as school lets out!"

"That's wonderful, darling," my mother had beamed.

"Of course, we'll have to discuss this first." Dad was a lawyer, and he never let a single detail go by. "How much would you be earning?"

"You'll never *believe* this!" Christine said dramatically.

"Twenty dollars an hour," was Mom's guess.

"Nope."

"Thirty," Dad had said.

"Uh-uh."

"Forty."

"You're not even close!"

"Fifty?"

"Getting warmer."

"Sixty."

"No, higher."

"Now, honey," Dad had protested. "If you go too much higher, you'll be out-earning me!" His eyes had twinkled in amusement.

"Seventy-five?" my mother asked, a little breathlessly.

"Not quite," Christine had answered with a triumphant grin. *"One hundred dollars an hour!"*

At first there was dead silence. Then both my parents started asking questions at once. "What kind of clothes will you be modeling, sweetheart?" my mother wanted to know.

Before Christine could answer, I'd interjected, "Invisible clothes."

Suddenly everyone turned to me, puzzled.

"What do you mean, 'invisible'?" Christine had scowled.

"Invisible clothes," I'd repeated. "They're invisible because they don't exist. You made it all up."

"I did not!"

"You did so."

"And how do you know? You weren't even there!"

"Maybe not, but I know enough about modeling to know you can't get a job just like that. Anybody knows that first you have to be formally accepted by the agency, and then they send you out on interviews. And even then you can't be sure of getting work!"

"Oh, yeah?" Realizing I had read up on the subject, Christine knew she'd been defeated. But giving up wasn't her style. "Why would Ms. Newson have bothered then? Besides, I know I have the right qualifications."

"You think you have the right qualifications for everything," I had retorted. "That's your problem!"

"That's *your* problem. You're just jealous!"

"I'm not jealous! I'm just trying to prevent you from wasting your time, that's all!"

"Ha! You just don't want me to be famous!"

We went on and on, until Mom and Dad had banged on the table with their forks and knives in an effort to make us stop. Thinking back on it as I reached in the closet for my shoes, I realized how silly we must have sounded. Just like little kids, arguing about shovels and pails at the beach, or swings in the playground, or new dresses in the store, or the largest piece of pie at home. Argue—that's all my sister and I ever seemed capable of doing. Except for that one year of togetherness as preteens, we just couldn't seem to stop being jealous and competitive.

I corrected myself: *I* couldn't stop being jealous and competitive. There was nothing about me for Christine to be jealous of. She was the one who had everything—good looks, popularity, boyfriends, a winning manner (at least, with *other* kids) and even acting talent. I suspected that even my parents probably secretly preferred her to me.

When I thought of Mom and Dad, an unexpected feeling of sympathy came over me. In spite of everything, I knew it must be awful for them to have two daughters who did nothing but fight. Feeling just a little sheepish, I made a resolution. If turning sixteen didn't help me become beautiful or popular with boys, there was one thing I *could* do on my birthday. I would try to get along better with my sister—no matter how much it hurt. I'd try to make turning sixteen just a little sweeter—if not for me, then at least for my parents.

If only Christine wasn't so irritable and unfriendly these days. I frowned, remembering how unapproachable she'd become. Could something possibly be bothering *her* too? No, I decided, grabbing my school books and running out the door. How could Christine have any problems?

Chapter Three

It was one of those typical late-fall mornings. The sky was clear and spring-like, but the air was quite cold. I squinted into the biting wind as I crossed Midland Avenue about halfway to school. My birthday would have to fall in one of the worst months of the year, I thought. In November, all I had to look forward to was a long, cold winter with lots of homework. To make matters worse, the trees were bare, the landscape was gray, and it got dark outside almost by the time I got home from school. It would be just my luck to be born on the dreariest day of the year! I was convinced that being born on November 1 had a lot to do with my being redheaded and average-looking. After all, Christine, who was born in sunny

17

June, was blonde and beautiful. As soon as I thought about Christine, I stopped myself. No more comparisons, I told myself. Think about something else!

So I turned to the only other subject worth thinking about—boys. I sorted through my mental file of the Northdale junior class and came up wanting. It wasn't that there weren't any decent guys around, but when you subtracted the boys who were going steady and those who were under 5'9" (my height) all that were left were creepy Richie types.

Of course, Christine never had problems like this. She could get any boy she wanted. Her latest, Jim Hoog, was our football team's quarterback. He had nice sandy blond hair, pale blue eyes, and muscular shoulders. And he was tan, even in the middle of autumn. He looked more like a California surfer than a teenager from a Chicago suburb! Christine, in one of her rare confiding moods, once told me that Jim went to a tanning salon. I believed it. He was so concerned about his looks, I was surprised he'd even play a rough sport like football!

I made a right turn at Green Avenue and soon found myself on the grounds of Northdale High. The school parking lot was bustling with activity; hundreds of kids were getting off the rickety old school buses, pulling up in cars or on bikes or just walking like myself. I wondered if there were other kids who secretly hated school and wished they weren't here, the way I often did. I looked at a group of boys wistfully. Most of them really weren't my type, but I couldn't help wishing that one of them, just *one*, would walk up to me and ask me for a date.

"Cynthia!" I heard someone call. I turned to see my best friend, Helen, running toward me.

"Why in the world did you call me Cynthia?" I demanded when she caught up to me.

"I bet you were dreaming about boys, again!" she teased.

"So? What does that have to do with anything?"

"When you're daydreaming, 'Cynthia' attracts your attention better than 'Cindy.'" She giggled. "I knew you'd snap right out of it, like when Mr. Boman catches you not paying attention in math class. If he gets you today, you're *through*. Even if it is your birthday."

I glared at her.

But if she noticed it, she ignored it. "I just wanted to wish you a happy birthday, Cin," she said.

"Thanks, Helen," I answered glumly.

"Hey, what's wrong?"

"Nothing."

Helen peered at me. "Bet I know," she said. "It's your birthday and you don't have a boyfriend to celebrate with."

In spite of my mood I laughed. "Boy, I can't keep anything from you, can I?" Helen had been my best friend for five years. She knew me better than almost anyone.

We headed for the back entrance to the school. "Look, Cindy, it's not hopeless, you know. Look at me and what happened when I turned sixteen."

"So you've had three more dates than I have. Big deal."

As soon as I said it, I was sorry. Helen had had as bad luck with boys as I had and her being slightly overweight hadn't helped matters any. But in the three months since she'd reached the magic age, a few boys in our class had begun to notice her. Even so, her limited dating experience had been less than totally successful. She was still looking for a real boyfriend, like I was.

"Hey, I didn't mean that, Helen," I told her. "Let's go to the mall after school, okay?"

"Sure," she said, brightening.

At that point we went our separate ways to our lockers. The beginning of another average day, I thought. Nothing even hinted at the fact that it wasn't going to be average at all—or that I wouldn't be able to keep my date with Helen.

Chapter Four

The morning periods were boring, as usual. Mr. Boman nearly put me to sleep, droning on in his dull monotone about permutations. It was a good thing Helen was there to keep my daydreaming in line.

Then the school day was half over, and I was headed for study period. It was held in the large auditorium by the back entrance of the school next to the cafeteria. Freshmen, sophomores, juniors, and seniors all sat together in seats assigned by the study teacher.

That's how it happened that Ron Peters, who was a senior, sat right behind me, a junior. He was one of the reasons why I liked study hall. Tall and cute, with straight brown hair that often flopped into his eyes, he was one of the most desirable boys in the school. Last year he had been the star of the basketball team, leading it to a second place finish in the regionals. I'd heard he wasn't on the team this year because he'd hurt his knee.

I knew all about this from Christine, of course. She'd babbled on and on about Ron after he joined the Drama Club. She described how funny he was and what a good actor he could be so many times that I'd often wondered why she didn't dump Jim for him. I certainly would have. But boys like Ron were attainable only in my daydreams. Even though he sat behind me, I was sure he didn't even know my name. I wondered what Ron would think if he knew I included him in my dreams sometimes. I smiled to myself as I took my seat in front of him. Wouldn't he be shocked to find out! Then again, he probably wouldn't care...

The bell rang, marking the beginning of forty-five minutes of quiet studying. I opened my geology book and tried to read, but it was hard. Ron, sitting behind me, was shuffling his long legs, tapping his pen and breathing down my neck! I was so conscious of him that once again, my homework ended up lying there in front of me—I stared at it with my eyes, but I couldn't concentrate. My mind was totally tuned into him.

I'd reached the point where I could figure out what he was doing just by the sounds he made. For example, if he was having trouble with a math problem, I'd hear a deep sigh—and I'd feel warm air blowing on the back of my neck, as if someone had opened a window in back of the room and let in a strong breeze. If he was writing an essay, I'd hear the steady tapping of his pen on his desk as he thought of what to write next. Then there was the shuffling of feet. Like I said, Ron was tall. Feeling cramped in his chair, he would change his foot positions at a rate of three times a minute (I timed him once). It was the kind of activity that would have annoyed me if Ron had been just anybody. But because he wasn't, the noises only reminded me of his presence and sent me off into wild study hall fantasies of what it would be like to be his girlfriend.

On this day, just as I was about to get back to my geology reading, Ron stretched his long legs under my seat and I felt a sharp kick on the back of my foot.

"Ow!" I yelled, more surprised than hurt. Miss O'Toole, the supervisor, gave me a warning look. I knew exactly what it meant: the first look was always a warning, the second was sure to mean detention. I was convinced she was the only teacher in the state of Illinois who gave out detentions for the simple act of talking.

"Hey, are you okay?" It was Ron, whispering to me. I had listened to his pencil tappings, foot-shufflings, and deep sighs since the beginning of the school year, but this was the first time he'd ever actually spoken to me.

"Uh-huh." I nodded, still looking in Miss O'Toole's direction. In her late forties, Miss O'Toole had deep furrows between her eyes and around her mouth that made her look as if she was always frowning in disapproval. Her dark, graying hair was pulled back into a knot, and she wore no makeup except for an outdated shade of red lipstick. She looked completely forbidding.

"Isn't she too much?" Ron's voice in my ear sounded husky and soft, as if he was confiding something special to me.

I tried very hard to keep cool, but it was hard. I could hardly believe that Ron and I were really having a conversation!

"Look at the way she stares out over the hall like that," I said. "It's enough to make you nervous."

"You know why she does it?" Ron asked.

"Sure, to keep us quiet."

"Yeah, but there's another reason."

"What is it?" I felt flattered that Ron wanted to pursue the subject.

"Well, I had her last year for American History, and I found out this secret about her," Ron whispered.

I couldn't resist turning halfway around in my seat to get a better look at him as he spoke. He was even cuter close up than he was on the basketball court. A lock of tousled dark hair fell over his forehead, and his eyes were the most incredible brown I had ever seen.

"She's deaf in one ear," he revealed.

I hardly heard what he said—I was staring so hard at his beautiful white teeth, and his smiling mouth. Suddenly the smile turned into a frown, and I heard him say, "Turn around, she's looking this way!"

I twisted back quickly into my seat, but it was too late.

"Cynthia Halley and Ron Peters—report to study hall after school." Miss O'Toole's sharp eyes were looking straight at me.

I sat back in my seat and groaned. It was bad enough that I would have to stay after school. Now Ron was sure to be furious at me for getting him into trouble.

A hundred pairs of eyes stared at us from around the study hall. They must be shocked, I thought, that Ron Peters, drama star and star pupil, had gotten caught!

I felt warm breath against my hair again, and Ron's voice whispered softly in my ear, "Well, I guess you got back at me for kicking you!"

This time I was too nervous and embarrassed to say anything. Besides, I wasn't going to take any more chances. It was strange though—when I looked at Miss O'Toole again, her frown was gone and the lines in her face had softened. In a funny way, she almost looked like an angel—a guardian angel who had helped bring Ron and me together.

At 3:00, when the rest of the student body of Northdale High was slamming locker doors shut, crowding into buses and running down the road away from school, Ron Peters and I returned to the study hall to receive punishment for our "crime." Miss O'Toole had gone home, and in her place was another teacher, Mr. Barker, who seemed very anxious to leave. He handed us exam booklets, as soon as we came in, and told us to write a 500-word essay on "Why I Must Not Talk."

After about two minutes of writing, he interrupted us to say, "Make that a 300-word essay." He seemed to feel worse than the kids did about having to stay after school!

Although he sat directly across the aisle from me, Ron didn't say a word during the detention. I looked up from my work once or twice only to see him busily writing away. The thought entered my mind that he might have a girlfriend waiting somewhere, maybe even a girl from another school. I knew that he had broken up with Gail Berry, his steady girl, a while ago. Since the beginning of this school year, he didn't seem to be dating anyone else in particular. He was ready for another girlfriend...

But as soon as I began to dream about Ron and me, I heard a little voice inside my head. *"Stupid!"* it scolded, *"whatever gives you the idea that you have a chance with Ron? He's one of the most popular boys in school, and you're a nobody. He certainly can't be interested in your looks. Look at your mousy red hair and your tall, skinny figure. You look like a boy."* I crossed out a sentence in my essay and frowned bitterly. That "little voice" inside of me was always spoiling everything.

"Cindy?" Ron suddenly broke into my thoughts. He was now standing in front of me.

"Huh . . . What?" I was startled. Had he seen my frown a minute before?

Ron's face smiled down at me. "Did you finish your essay? We're allowed to leave when we're finished."

"Oh, yeah, sure," I answered hastily. "I finished a while ago. I was just thinking."

"Thinking about how badly behaved you were in study hall, right?" he teased.

"Me? It was all your fault, for kicking me!" I answered, smiling.

"How was I supposed to know you keep your feet there?"

"Where am I supposed to keep my feet?" I protested. "In Miss O'Toole's lap?"

"Well, anyway, you didn't have to yell. I didn't kick that hard."

"Oh, no?" I pointed at Ron's shoes playfully. "Did you ever take a look at the size of your feet?"

Ron looked at his large jogging sneakers. "No, not lately, now that you mention it," he admitted, chuckling. Then looking at me, he added, "Since you're such a weakling, how about a ride home? I can drop you off on my way to work."

"Gee, thanks. It's the least you can do." I tried

to sound casual. But in fact, my heart was beating so hard, I was afraid the "thump-thump-thump" would show under my sweater.

Gathering our things, we handed our essays in to Mr. Barker and walked out of the school building and into the parking lot. A couple of kids hanging out by a shiny red Camaro looked over at Ron and me curiously. One of them called out, "How's it going, Ron?" He waved back cheerfully, and I felt really proud to be seen with him.

When he got to his car, a slightly beat-up Mustang, Ron said, "It's open," so I got in on the passenger side and slid into the seat.

As Ron got in on the other side behind the wheel and started the car, I began to daydream again. This time I fantasized that Ron Peters was my date, and that it was Saturday and we were going somewhere together. I looked at his mouth again, the way I had in study hall, and imagined what it would be like if he kissed me...

"What in the world are you thinking about?" Stunned, I turned to see Ron looking at me curiously. Then he made a right turn out of the school grounds.

"Oh, I was just trying to figure out this math problem I have for homework," I lied, hoping the color on my face didn't give me away.

"That bad, huh?" Ron asked, smiling as he made a left turn past the gas station near our school.

"What's bad?" I asked apprehensively. Had he noticed how self-conscious I was?

"I mean, you really are a serious student, aren't you?"

"How could you tell?" I asked him. *Had he noticed me before today?* I could hardly believe that.

Ron watched the road in front of him, sweeping the hair back off his forehead. "I've been watching you in study hall lately. You concentrate so hard on your homework that nothing seems to distract you. That's why I kicked you. I had to make sure you were really alive."

"Are you saying that you kicked me on purpose?" I pretended to be mad, but I was ecstatic.

Ron glanced over at me. "Actually, I was getting tired of looking at the back of your head. The front view is a lot better."

"Why, thank you," I said, pleased. The idea that Ron had kicked me on purpose really threw me. Ron was a bigshot at school. He could have any girl he wanted to. What did he want from *me*?

We turned into the driveway. Before I could thank Ron for the ride and jump out of the car, he stopped me.

"Not so fast." He grabbed the sleeve of my blue down jacket and held on to it.

"What?" I turned back and looked at him behind the wheel, holding my sleeve and looking as cool as could be.

"Do you think your foot'll be healed by tomorrow night?"

"My foot?" I asked, dazed. "Sure. Why?"

"How about if I pick you up at seven? There's supposed to be a good movie over by the mall, and..."

Ron was suggesting a date. I heard him, but I couldn't believe it. I felt like one of my daydreams had gone haywire, like it was running on without my being able to control it. Then I remembered that when a boy asked you out, you were supposed to say something.

"Uh...yeah...I mean...uh...sure, great," I mumbled awkwardly. "Seven's fine. See you tomorrow."

The flirtatious manner I had managed to keep up in study hall had all but vanished, and in its place, the real me returned—the awkward shy, unpoised me that I never intended to let Ron see. Instantly, I became furious at myself. Why did I have to behave so stupidly?

But Ron didn't seem to notice. "Seven it is," he said, adding, "Now I'd better get going! I work at Mayfield's after school, and I'm already more than an hour late."

With that, he put his car into reverse and backed down the driveway. Then he waved one last time and drove off, leaving me with shaking legs.

A moment later I looked up to see my sister Christine standing about a block up the street with the two small children she baby-sat after school. Ron stopped the car to chat with her, and I felt my heart stand still for a moment. What were they talking about? Would he tell Christine about our date? What would she think? I prayed she wouldn't say anything negative about me, something that might change Ron's mind about taking me out. Then I scolded myself: "Christine's not that bad. She'd never be that malicious. They're probably talking about the Drama Club."

Still, the old fear gripped me and held me fast. Would Ron have asked me out if Christine wasn't going with Jim Hoog? Was I just a second choice, the younger, plainer sister of a family of two girls? I forced these thoughts out of my mind. Ron had asked *me* for a date on Saturday! And nothing was going to change that.

I saw Ron speed off in the distance, leaving Christine alone with the two kids. Suddenly my mood lifted sky high. Sixteen was turning out to be sweet after all. I had a date with Ron Peters!

Still shaking slightly, I took out my key and let myself into the house. I felt so happy as I wiped my feet and took off my coat that it hardly even occurred to me that Ron had known, without my telling him, the exact route to my house.

Chapter Five

I felt the strangest sensation as I entered the living room. It was the same old house, but for some reason everything looked different, clearer and brighter. Things stood out more than they did before.

Suddenly I found myself drawn to a painting that hung over the TV set. It had been there for as long as I could remember, but I had never really looked at it before. Today it was like a magnet, pulling me. It was a painting of the English countryside in springtime. Gentle green hills rolled on to the horizon, sprinkled with the first yellow, pink and purple wildflowers of spring. The sky was a soft, bright blue, spotted here and there with fluffy clouds. Gazing at the painting, I could almost smell the flowers and feel myself running ankle-deep in lush, moist grass.

"Oh, Cindy, I didn't hear you come in. How do you like it?" Mom's question broke my reverie.

"I love it!" I turned to smile at her. "I never got close enough before to get a good look at it..."

"What do you mean?" My mother looked puzzled. "We only got it today."

"We did?" Now it was my turn to be puzzled. "I swear it's been here before, but I never really noticed it."

"Never noticed it! You can't see the forest for the trees. If Dad and I didn't limit your TV watching, you'd be staring at it twenty-four hours a day! But don't you remember the old set broke down? This is a new one."

"Oh, the TV!" Finally realizing what my mother meant, I burst out laughing. "I thought you were talking about the painting."

Now Mom laughed, too. Then she stopped and looked at me. "Are you sure you're feeling all right?"

I could feel my face getting hot. I wasn't ready to tell Mom about Ron yet. "I'm fine," I answered guiltily, turning back to the painting before she could see my blush. "Where'd you get this painting, anyway?"

Fortunately, Mom didn't seem to notice anything funny. "When I first fell in love with your father, I noticed it in a shop." She smiled, eager to tell me the story. "I bought it for his birthday... you never noticed it before?"

"Oh, Mom, you know how things are."

"Sure," she said, letting the matter drop. "Come into the kitchen. I've got a surprise for you."

I realized then what that wonderful aroma in the air was. In the kitchen, I saw a huge, creamy chocolate cake, complete with sixteen candles. My birthday cake!

"Mom!" I protested. "You don't have a hundred people hiding in closets ready to spring out at me, do you?"

"Don't worry, Cindy. I'm not going to force you to have a party. On the other hand..." She smiled. "...I wasn't going to let you deprive me of baking my favorite cake. So how about a private celebration?"

She took out two glasses and poured us some fruit punch. Holding our glasses in the air, we made a toast.

"Here's to a terrific mother!" I said, clinking my glass with hers.

"And here's to a super daughter on her sixteenth birthday," my mother said. Then she lit the candles on the cake and ordered, "Now make a wish and blow!"

I blew out the candles and then Mom cut two big pieces of the cake. Luckily, she didn't ask me what my wish was. She would have been shocked to find out that I suddenly hoped people *would* jump out of closets!

But party or no party, nothing was more important to me than my date with Ron on Saturday night. Thinking about him put me in such a great mood that I was sure nothing could possibly make me feel sad again.

That feeling lasted all through the day, even at dinner time, in spite of Christine's new announcement.

"Hey, Mom, Dad," she said, "guess what happened to me today?"

My parents looked up from their soup. "What, dear?" they replied in unison.

Christine spoke triumphantly. "I got ninety-nine on my math test. But that isn't even the best part."

She paused, waiting just long enough so Mom could say, "Go on, honey."

"Mr. Bert, my math teacher, said that nobody else in the *entire* five years he's been in Northdale High has gotten a mark even *close* to ninety-nine on that particular exam!"

Meanwhile my sister stole a glance at me as if to dare me to say something. But I held fast. Don't forget the resolution, I reminded myself silently.

"That's wonderful, sweetheart!" said my father. "If you ever change your mind about modeling you can come and be my personal accountant."

"I don't know where you get your math skills, Christine," Mom added, obviously impressed.

"Nobody else in the family shows a bit of talent in math..." She paused, leaving the sentence dangling in mid-air, obviously thinking of my reaction to that remark.

I couldn't really blame her. Any other day, I would've snapped, "Who cares how you do in dumb old math." But today I was going to stick to my plan. "That's super, Christine!" I told her. "I couldn't come *close* to that!"

I wasn't prepared for the way my response surprised my parents. They were both so stunned that their spoons were left poised over their soup. Christine, too, stared at me in amazement. It occurred to me for a moment that she might even have enjoyed our fights. After all, they'd become such a habit. But one look at my parents' faces told me that it was one habit they'd like to see broken for good.

Later that evening, after Christine had left on a date, I had another piece of birthday cake with my parents. As we were eating, my father said, "By the way, do you have anything to tell us, Cindy?"

I looked at him guiltily. Was he referring to Ron? Could he tell?

"You met a boy today, didn't you?" Mom's eyes peered over the rim of her coffee cup. They were teasing, but kind. Had Christine said something to them?

"Well, yes. How did you know?" I asked nervously.

"Christine was sure you were running in to tell me about it when you came home," Mom said.

I looked down at my plate.

"Do you want to tell us about him?" Mom prodded gently.

"His name's Ron Peters, a guy at school," I said. "He's real nice, handsome, pretty popular. Christine knows him. He's in the Drama Club. So...is it all right for me to go out with him tomorrow night?"

I was so afraid my parents might say "no" that I blocked out their answer.

"Of course you can, Cindy," said my father.

I looked up at him, protesting, "Why not? He's really nice...please?"

"I said yes, Cindy," Dad repeated. "Why in the world do you think we'd say no? As long as you say he's nice and reliable, we trust you. Besides, Christine told us all about him."

"She did?" I looked up suspiciously. "Look, I promise you'll never be sorry you let me date Ron," I told my parents as I kissed them in gratitude. "Thanks, Mom, Dad...I..."

Instead of saying anything, my parents sat there smiling, looking first at each other, then at me, then back to each other. They wore the same grin I imagined they must have had when I spoke my first word or took my first step or ate my first bite of solid food. Now I felt embarrassed again. Parents could sure be corny sometimes! This was only going to be my first date. I froze on that thought. *My first date*—the words sounded so good in my mind.

A noise outside my window roused me from a deep sleep that night. It was probably Christine, returning from her date with Jim. Sleepily I glanced over to my clock-radio. The green numbers read 2:00 A.M. Would Mom and Dad know that Christine had violated her curfew?

I thought for a moment of blackmailing her, but then changed my mind. I lay back in bed, peering into the still darkness of my room. It was funny how different I felt now that I had a date. I used to feel so jealous whenever I heard Christine coming home late at night. And now I didn't. Envy really did have a lot to do with my own emptiness and insecurity, I thought. It didn't really have much to do with Christine at all . . .

"Christine," I heard a voice below my window say, "you're mine. You have to tell him."

Wow, I thought. I didn't know Jim had it in him to be so romantic. But who was "him"?

Slipping out of bed, I crept silently toward the window. Then pulling myself up at the window ledge, I peered into the darkness. I felt a little guilty, but I figured what Christine and Jim didn't know wouldn't hurt them. Besides, I told myself, I have to see how kissing is done. What if Ron tried to kiss me tomorrow night, and I didn't even know how?

I saw the silhouette of two figures standing on the doorstep below. Christine's bright hair shone in the moonlight, but Jim's didn't reflect any light at all. Since his hair was almost the same color as Christine's, that struck me as a bit odd.

I leaned over to get a better look. Jim's arms were around Christine's shoulders, holding her tight. Her arms were clasped around his back. His mouth was pressed on hers, and the two of them were locked in a long, passionate kiss. The sight filled me with longing. I'd always wanted to be kissed like that, but until now, I could only dream about it. Would my dream come true with Ron?

"When will I see you again?" Jim kissed Christine on the nose, and then all over her face.

"I don't know. I don't know." I watched my sister hold her face up in ecstasy, while Jim kissed her neck. I made a mental note to remember that one. It looked good. But Christine's words were so odd. Why didn't she know? Didn't she see Jim every day in school? Was she just acting again?

"Please . . . soon," Jim was saying. "Tell . . . goodbye. I . . . you." I strained to hear better, but a passing car blocked out some of the words. "Tell who goodbye?" I wondered. This was getting bizarre.

I watched as they kissed one last time. Then Jim let go and walked away toward the car. Christine took a key from her leather bag and turned it in the front door lock. Before she entered the house, I saw Jim turn back to look at her. For an instant the moonlight caught his dark, angular features. I gasped. It wasn't Jim at all! But who was it?

I scurried back to bed, pulling the blue goose-down filled quilt way over my face. When I heard Christine coming up the steps in the hall, I held my breath. She paused for a minute by my door, then went to her room at the end of the hall. Did she suspect I'd been watching? She had caught me once, two years ago, when I was fourteen. The window shade had flipped up while I watched her and Stanley Morris, her steady in the tenth grade. I grinned. Her kissing had sure improved a lot since then! But who was this strange new boyfriend of hers? Where was Jim? Still wondering, I rearranged myself under the quilt and fell asleep.

Chapter Six

The sun was streaming into the room when I awoke the next morning. Lazily I lay watching the different shapes and designs the bright rays made on the floor and walls of my room. Catching my paperweight prism, the rays scattered an assortment of rainbow colors all over my desk.

I stretched and snuggled deeper into my feather pillows. There was nothing like Saturday morning! No jumping up at 6:45 to get ready for school, no dressing in the dark, no last-minute cramming for exams before running out of the house. No nothing! Gathering the blankets around me, I smiled...Saturday morning.

Saturday morning!

Suddenly I shot out of bed as if I'd been hit

on the head. Had I really forgotten? I had to get ready for my date with Ron! I had to decide on something to wear. Then, I had to wash and style my hair, and that could take *hours*. And most important, I had to think. What would I say to Ron? How would I act? What should I do? Standing on the cold floor, I shivered slightly.

I'd been out with groups of kids before, but never on a date. Were there rules I didn't know about? Should I just act as if Ron were only a friend, like Helen? Would he understand my having a curfew? Suddenly I felt totally perplexed. I wished someone would tell me what I should say, how I should act, even what I should wear.

When I got to the kitchen, I put the water on for my tea and popped two pieces of whole wheat bread in the toaster. Mom was already sitting at the table, her coffee cup in front of her as she read the paper. She hardly even noticed me.

"Mom, what was dating like when you were young?" I asked, catching her off guard. She'd been absorbed in the gossip column of the *Chicago Sun-Times*, even though she was always criticizing newspaper gossip as frivolous and a waste of space.

"Huh?" she said, looking slightly guilty.

"I saw you reading the gossip column," I teased.

"Nosey," she said, making a face. "Now what did you say?"

"What was dating like when you were young?" I repeated. "Was it a lot like it is today?"

"Dating?" My mother put down the paper and looked off as if deep in thought. "Umm, I don't know."

"Well, what was it like with Dad?"

"Very nice, thank you." Mom smiled. Then she said, "My parents were a lot stricter with me than Dad and I are with Christine. Of course, we trust her..."

"Didn't your parents trust you?" I felt puzzled. Imagine not trusting my own mother!

"Oh, yes!" Mom looked at me. "But in those days—boy, I make it sound so long ago!—people were very concerned with appearances. Grandma and Grandpa felt they had to protect me, and my reputation. Everyone in the neighborhood knew when I went out, who I went out with, and when I got back. If I stayed out too late, boy was I in trouble!"

"Ugh!" I made a face. Then I said, "But people still talk, today, don't they?"

"Oh, of course," she answered. "But it's not like it was. The neighbors don't peek out of windows any more to spy on the girl next door kissing her boyfriend."

My face turned pink. Maybe the neighbors didn't peek, but Mom would die if she knew I'd spied on Christine. When it came to modernization ratings, I sure pulled in a low score. But if Mom knew, she didn't let on, thank goodness.

I retrieved my tea and toast and ambled back to the table. "So describe dating with Dad," I suggested.

"Well, for starters, we saw each other only on weekend nights," she said.

"Only on weekends?" I gasped.

"Yes. Not counting seeing each other at school, that is."

"So what were your actual dates like?" I prodded. I couldn't imagine my parents dating the way Christine and Jim Hoog did.

"I looked forward to Friday night all week," Mom told me. "Then at exactly seven P.M., your father would ring the doorbell. Grandpa or Uncle Dave would answer the door while I would call down, 'I'll be right there.' I was never ready until five after seven. That gave your father a chance to talk to Grandpa for a while."

"It sounds so *formal*! Didn't you just want to run out the door with him?"

Mom smiled. "Sure. But I had rules to follow. Like I said, your grandparents were very strict with me. But your father was concerned about my feelings and knew I had to follow the rules. I wasn't afraid to introduce him to my parents because he was so good and sensitive, and smart. I just knew they'd love him. And look where we are now." She turned to me, as if asking for my confirmation.

"But Mom—only weekend nights?" I persisted. "Didn't you want to date Dad more often?"

She got up to pour herself another cup of

coffee. "Well, we did, eventually, after we became engaged. But I'll tell you a secret." My mother's eyes twinkled, looking exactly the same shade of blue as the bright morning sky outside. "Those Friday and Saturday nights were extra special. They made my whole week. I'll never forget that feeling of anticipation—and I was never let down. Sometimes I think kids today are too free. They lose so much in terms of anticipation. Take Christine, for example..."

"What about Christine?" I asked.

"Oh, never mind," Mom said, putting down her coffee cup. And as if reading my mind she added, "Don't worry about tonight, Cindy. Just be yourself and concentrate on having a good time." She looked up at me with her "end of conversation" look and went back to the paper.

Quickly I finished breakfast and went back upstairs, still puzzled and confused and excited. Christine was awake now. She was in the bathroom we shared. The door was open and I stood staring at her for a minute, wondering if I dared ask her about what was on my mind. She was in the midst of her morning ritual—putting gobs of makeup on her cheeks and eyes. What would Jim say if he saw her now? Would he still think she was so beautiful? And what about that other boy she was with last night? Did I dare ask her about *that*?

"What are you staring at?" Christine eyed me, as if she knew what I was thinking.

"Oh, nothing," I lied, toying with the pins

and clips in the jar labeled "MISC." "I was just wondering."

"Wondering what?" She reached for a long makeup brush and began to apply contour powder under her cheekbones.

"What's it like to date?" There, I'd finally asked her. Funny, it was harder to ask Christine than my mother. And my sister was from my own generation.

"Why, are you afraid you're gonna screw things up with Ron tonight?" Without missing a beat she reached for her coral-tinted blush.

"Well—um—no, of course not!" There was no way I was going to admit my insecurity to her now. I could tell she was not going to be sympathetic.

"So, what about it? There's nothing to know. Just go out, that's all. What's the big deal?"

"I was just wondering, that's all," I said, trying to sound as casual as she did. "Say, are there any kind of 'rules' I should know about?" I pretended to be absorbed in a safety pin.

"Rules!" Christine scoffed. Boy, was she making it hard.

"Well, Mom says there were rules when she went out with Dad." I switched to cleaning my fingernails with a file.

Christine laughed. I looked at my hands unhappily. Weren't older sisters supposed to be *helpful*?

"That's Mom and Dad, stupid," she said. "That was *years* ago. Things change, you know."

"So what is changed, smarty-pants?" I bent the file out of shape.

"Smarty-pants!" She pointed her hairbrush at me. "What does that mean—'smarty-pants'? You know, you're going to have to start getting a little more sophisticated, Cin."

I yelled back at her in frustration. "So stop giving me a hard time and just tell me what you're supposed to do on a date!"

Christine put down the brush. Suddenly she was serious, too. "There's nothing much to tell," she said. "You just go out, that's all. Just go and be yourself."

I was more confused than ever. Both Mom and Christine told me to "act natural." But what did that mean? If I just acted like myself, I'd either be so eager that I'd be all over Ron, or I'd be so scared that I'd be hiding behind a chair. No, I couldn't act naturally. Not yet, anyway.

If I didn't know how to act, at least I could look right, I told myself as I headed back to my room. I was rummaging through my closet, trying to figure out what to wear, when I heard a knock on my bedroom door.

"Morning, sleepyhead!" Helen's brown curls appeared behind the door as it opened a crack.

"What are you doing here so early?" I looked first at Helen, then at the clock. It was 10:30, eight and one-half hours before Ron would pick me up. "You're never up and around until way after noon."

"Oh, yeah?" Helen's merry brown eyes twinkled with mischief. "Look who didn't even make her bed yet." She walked into the room and plunked down into my rocker. "You didn't think I'd let you down on a day like this, did you? How are you holding up?"

"Oh, Helen!" I wailed, glad that someone understood me. "What am I going to wear? You've got to help me."

"That bad, huh?" She looked me up and down. "What's wrong with your overalls?"

"Are you serious?" I asked.

"No, I guess I'm not." She giggled. "Although Susan Werner and Steve Bates always go around in overalls."

"Helen, that's why everybody calls them the Bobbsey twins. Besides, they've been going together for years."

"Isn't that what you're after?"

"Oh, please! First I've just got to get through one night."

"What about one of your own creations?"

"Nah, not special enough." I liked to sew, but I hadn't made anything recently that I liked enough to wear on a date. "Help me pick out something quick!"

"Okay." Helen joined me at my closet. "Well, well, whatcha got?" She held up an old antique print dress that had belonged to my grandmother. It was something I'd wanted desperately at one time, but I hardly ever found an occasion to wear it.

"Forget it, Helen," I said. "Too old-fashioned."

"Now what's this?" She held up a red silk dress from China and whistled. "Wow, this must be real form-fitting."

"Yep. My aunt got that for me in Hong Kong. It's great to look at, but you can't move for fear of ripping it. Forget it."

Next, she brought out a tailored tweed suit. I'd bought that on impulse, believing people would take me more seriously if I wore it. Instead they handed me job applications.

"Too stuffy," I complained.

"Wear it when you want to mind Ron's business."

"Ha, ha. You get a 'three' for that one." And so we went on. Piece by piece, we examined every single blouse, pants, sweater, and jacket in my closet. Some things were too small, others were out-of-style, and most were just not special enough.

Finally, Helen pulled out my yellow cowl neck sweater. "Here it is! It's perfect!"

"I can't, Helen," I moaned. "That's what I wore yesterday when Ron asked me out!"

"You see, there *is* magic to that sweater," Helen remarked. She put it down and picked up a blue striped V-neck. "How about this?"

"Christine's hand-me-down." I sighed. "He knows her, so he's sure to notice. Listen, this is just hopeless."

My friend looked at me sideways. "How much money have you got?"

"Why?"

"We're going to the mall. Come on, hurry up."

Leaving a pile of useless, discarded clothing strewn all over the room, off we went.

Chapter Seven

Mayfield Mall was a huge shopping center on the outskirts of Northdale. It had four big department stores, five shoe stores, three pet stores, twenty boutiques, two hardware stores, one garden center, and lots of candy stores, ice cream shops and restaurants. It was also the biggest hangout for miles around, drawing kids from Northdale and all the surrounding towns. Built to resemble a real town, it had walkways, bridges, canals, fountains, pools with goldfish and false fronts to make the buildings look authentic. To us kids it was a make-believe town, full of wonderful things to buy and places to visit.

Only on this Saturday it just wasn't quite as much fun as it usually was. I was under too much pressure to get that perfect sweater or blouse for my date with Ron. The trouble was that the ideal top had to be a lot of things. It had to be pretty, but not too far-out. It had to be colorful, but not flamboyant. Sexy, but not sleazy. Special, but not crazy. Comfortable, but not dumpy. Inexpensive, but not cheap looking. Helen and I searched through the four department stores and all twenty boutiques and . . . nothing. There was nothing perfect enough to buy.

"Let's go see what's happening in the hardware store," Helen suggested after three hours of sweater-hunting. We'd just finished lunch, and, standing outside the hamburger shop, we were trying to decide on our next move.

"Why, what's in hardware?" I asked, puzzled.

"Not what—who."

"You mean a boy, don't you?"

"You hit the nail on the head," she giggled.

"A 'five' for that one," I said. "On target, but overused."

"Well, you want to go talk to him?"

"Who?"

"Jason Greenberg."

"Jason Greenberg!" I made a face.

"What's wrong with him?" According to Helen, there wasn't much wrong with any boy, so long as he was male.

"Oh, he's okay, I guess. A little too conceited for my tastes, though. He came over to the house with Jim once after football practice and made a big deal about some passes he caught. You after him?"

Helen grabbed my arm and stared at me wide-eyed. "Call me, immediately."

"Huh?"

"Call me the minute he sets foot in your house again."

"Why?" I played dumb.

"Oh, Cindy. Give me a break, p-l-e-a-s-e. I'm in love with that guy. He's adorable!"

"Humph!" I snorted. "You hardly even know him. Anyway, what about his girlfriend . . . what's her name . . . Fay?"

"Finished," Helen said. "They broke up." She did a turn. "How do I look as runner-up?"

"As far as I'm concerned, he's no prize," I sniffed.

"So you won't come with me to see him?" Helen persisted. I studied her for a moment. She looked so determined I figured this time she might actually have a chance. But she didn't really need me tagging along.

I looked at my watch. "Uh-oh. I've got to get going! It's three o'clock already, and I haven't accomplished *anything* . . ."

"Oh, Cindy, honestly." Helen frowned. "I know what you're going through, but you're building it up way out of proportion. Lighten up. After all, it's only a date, and Ron's just human."

"I know, I know," I wailed. "I guess I'm paranoid. I don't know what to do. Maybe I'll just wear my plaid shirt...no, my white Victorian blouse...I mean, my navy blue..."

Helen shook my shoulders. "Relax, silly. You'll do just fine. After all, he asked *you*, didn't he?"

"Yeah, I forgot," I agreed. "He did ask me, didn't he? Now tell me he'll ask me out a second time, even if I mess up tonight."

"How can you mess up? If things don't work out, at least you'll be over the hurdle of your first date."

"Helen!"

"What?"

"That sounds awful!"

"Why?"

"You're supposed to say that Ron and I will live happily ever after."

Helen smiled and swung her arm across the sky, taking in the mall and the whole world behind it in one sweep. "And miss all those gorgeous boys out there? Are you crazy?"

I laughed. "I haven't even got one yet, and you're trying to sell me on the whole population!"

She pushed a dark curl out of her eye. "That's right!" she said emphatically. "I know you don't want to hear this now, but there's a whole world out there, Cin, and we're just beginning!"

"You sound like my mother," I replied dryly. "Like when I took my first step."

"Want to know something, Cin?"

"What?"

"Dating is a lot more fun than walking."

"Okay, expert," I answered. "But doesn't it also hurt more when you fall?"

"Sure, but then you wait around for the next boy to come along and pick you up."

"Oh, come on! What kind of life is that?" I huffed. "Going from boy to boy as if nothing else mattered."

"You've just gone from store to store as if nothing else mattered. And all for a boy!"

I knew she was right. "Okay, you got me. No more stores. I'm putting on the first thing I see when I get home."

"So come and visit Jason with me," Helen said. "You can practice flirting with him. I won't mind."

"No," I joked. "You'll just wait until I win him over—"

"And then sneak back to your house and wait for Ron to show up at seven." Helen finished for me. "No thanks, Cin, Ron's okay, but he's not my type."

"Good!" I said. With that I waved goodbye and left for home, while Helen headed for Jason.

The rest of the afternoon was a near-disaster. When I got home I washed my hair twice to make it extra clean, but instead it got so tangled up and fly-away, I had to condition it for twenty minutes. Then I couldn't decide whether to wear real or designer jeans. In our school, some kids wore Levi's while others wore the designer kind. I decided Ron was definitely a

"Levi's" type. Unfortunately, my Levi's were dirty, and I hadn't remembered to wash them. So I ended up running the washer and dryer just for them, and Mom yelled at me for wasting so much water and electricity.

Then of course there was Christine. I got into another fight with her when she caught me using her makeup. I thought I'd look a little more grown-up if I wore some eye-liner and blush, but she exploded when she saw me dabbling with *her* personal stuff. But it didn't really matter. I ended up looking so terrible that I took it right off again.

At about 5 P.M. and three arguments later, Dad said he was going to call off the date if it was going to cause so much disruption in the household. Of course he was kidding, but I got the point and tried to calm down. I even apologized to Christine, and she was so shocked that she offered to do my hair. The last time Christine had bothered to touch my hair was when she braided my pigtails in the fifth grade. But this time, she made a really sophisticated-looking style by twisting the sides of my hair up and back. She even let me borrow her barrettes to fasten the whole thing together.

Then Mom got into the act. She let me wear her pink mohair sweater with the scoop neck. My gold necklace and bangle bracelets completed the outfit.

By about 6 P.M., I finally had it all together. Then Jim Hoog appeared to take Christine out on their date. After they left, I was alone with Mom and Dad. Since Ron wasn't due for another fifteen minutes, all there was left for me to do was wait . . .

Chapter Eight

"I thought we'd go to a movie," Ron said, smoothing his hair down with one hand while driving with the other. "Then we can go to Jack's Snacks afterward. Is that okay with you, Cindy?"

"Oh, it's fine," I answered. It wouldn't have made much difference if he had suggested going to the moon. All I cared about was that Ron was really here, I was really with him and we were really on a date!

"Oh, good." Ron grinned at me. "I was worried it wouldn't sound too exciting. But I'm sure your folks wouldn't be too thrilled if we took a trip into Chicago."

"No, they wouldn't," I answered, relieved. "I'm not even allowed to go to Chicago during the day to shop by myself. Dad thinks it's too dangerous."

"Oh, really?" Ron said, turning onto the highway. "Well, if you want to shop, there's always Mayfield's. What more could you ask for?"

I laughed, hoping I didn't sound too nervous. Inside, I felt as jittery as Jello. "Is that where we're going now?"

"Yep." Ron smiled. "All roads lead to Rome. Or, at least to 'Threatre.' There's a new comedy playing there tonight."

"Threatre" was the name of the movie theater in Mayfield Mall. The extra "r" wasn't a mistake—it was a play on "three," referring to the triple screens in the building.

"Oh, super." I sat back in my seat and stared at the strip of highway stretching out in front of us. What a stupid expression that was—"Oh, super." I played with my fingers as I felt a deadly silence enveloping us. Why couldn't I think of anything clever to say? I felt as if I must seem really dumb compared to the lively, talkative girls Ron knew from Drama Club. Like Christine, for instance...

"Do you like to read, Cindy?" Ron's question startled me.

"Oh, yes. Why? Do you?" I hated the way I sounded. Why couldn't I answer casually, the way I would've if Helen asked me the same thing? Anyway, what did Ron mean? Did he think I was a bookworm?

"I love reading!" Ron answered. "Even Shakespeare, though some kids I know think that's crazy. Have you ever read any Shakespeare?"

"Only *Hamlet*," I admitted. I didn't add that it was a school assignment, and that I found it difficult to keep my mind on it, though I knew it was supposed to be a classic.

"I didn't like Shakespeare much in the beginning," he went on, as if he'd read my mind. "But since I'm playing Romeo I started to read the stuff in depth, and you know—it really makes sense!"

"Romeo?" I sat up and looked at him, forgetting my shyness of a minute before. "When did they announce that? I didn't hear anything about it in school."

"Oh, darn!" Ron pressed a hand to his mouth. "You have to help me keep a secret, Cindy. I got the part, but I'm not supposed to know. I overheard the drama coach . . . and anyway, they're supposed to announce it on Monday. Do me a favor, okay? Don't spill the beans that I know."

"Of course not!" I said. Imagine Ron letting me in on a secret. I felt pleased and flattered.

"Who's going to be Juliet?" I asked timidly. We had approached the entrance to Mayfield's, and Ron stopped to make the turn.

"That one I didn't overhear," he replied. Fortunately, he didn't seem to notice my apprehension.

At Threatre, we met another couple, Bob Falmouth and Betsey White. They were both seniors, and for a moment I felt in awe of the group I was with. In our school, it was an honor to be included with the seniors. Bob and Betsey were so easy-going, however, that I soon forgot to be shy. I wondered if Ron had invited them on purpose on our first date? They were the kind of people who had such ready laughs and easy manners that it was impossible to be nervous around them. Pretty soon after the movie started I began to relax and enjoy myself.

Fortunately, the movie turned out to be as hilarious as Ron predicted. I don't know what kind of effect a really scary or sexy or serious movie would've had on me. As it was I felt good sitting so close to Ron. He wore an aftershave, and I knew I'd remember the scent for the rest of my life. Every once in a while he'd lean over to whisper something about the movie, and it was fantastic feeling him so close to me, with our shoulders almost touching, and his head next to mine.

When the movie let out, we agreed to meet Bob and Betsey a few minutes later at Jack's Snacks. Jack's had been the local hangout for kids from Northdale High for as long as I could remember, although people rarely went there without a date. Christine always mentioned "going to Jack's" as if it were the most everyday thing to do. But I had never gone for fear of being seen there alone, which would have been awful.

I felt another thrill of happiness as we rode to Jack's. Finally I would be taking part in some of the fun that was going on around me, instead of just sitting around on the sidelines. I wasn't going to be an outsider anymore. —

As if reading my thoughts, Ron put his arm around my shoulder. "How'd you like the movie?" He smiled and moved closer to me.

"It was super!" I managed to say. "Real funny!" Feeling myself against Ron's body made me go hot and cold all over. Did he realize what he was doing to me? Was he doing it on purpose? Did he feel the same way I did? I thought of Ron's other girlfriends, who were a lot sexier, and I guessed not.

A few minutes later, we pulled into Jack's parking lot. The place was jammed—it seemed the entire student body of Northdale High was there. Cars drove in and out of the lot, while packs of kids stood around everywhere, smoking, fooling around, and checking out cars and motorcycles. Running, shrieking girls nearly knocked us over as Ron and I entered the swinging doors.

Inside, the place was jumping. It sent a thrill through my spine to stand there with Ron—we were getting looked over by all the kids who were already seated. What must they think, I wondered, to see me, Cynthia Halley, with Ron Peters?

Shouts from the back of the restaurant interrupted my thoughts. Bob and Betsey had gotten there first and were saving a booth. As we made our way to the back, the guys who knew Ron held out their hands for him to slap, or simply said, "How's it going?" The girls looked at me curiously. I was glad I was wearing the pink mohair sweater. Only a day ago, it wouldn't have mattered, because I wouldn't have gotten a second look. But suddenly I was something special. For tonight, at least, I was Ron Peters' girl.

After we made our way to the booth, we ordered hamburgers and Cokes. Bob and Betsey were anxious to talk about the movie and even I had something to say.

"Well, fancy meeting you here!" A husky female voice broke into our conversation. I looked up to see a dark-haired girl who was wearing tight black jeans and a cashmere sweater. She had the most incredible figure I'd ever seen. Something about the way she tossed her thick, wavy hair and looked at Ron put me on guard. Who was she and what did she want?

I could feel Ron tense up slightly. "Hey, how are you?" he said, sounding uncomfortable.

Looking at the subdued looks on Bob's and Betsey's faces, I instantly realized who the girl was. Gail Berry. I had heard of Ron's old girlfriend by name, but I'd never seen her, since she attended Clairbrook High in the next town. Now that I had, I wanted to crawl into the woodwork. I was nothing compared to her.

"So what's new, sweetheart?" she went on. What business did she have calling my date "sweetheart"? I wondered furiously. My anger changed to confusion and fear as she leaned down and kíssed Ron on the forehead. He didn't seem to enjoy it, but I felt awful. A horrible thought struck me. What if Ron still loved her and wished he wasn't with me right now?

It was everything I could do not to disappear under the table. I wished I had the power to make myself invisible.

"And who is this?" Now Gail turned her attention to me. Her mouth was smiling, but her eyes looked cold and mean.

"Oh." Ron turned and looked toward me uneasily. "Cindy, this is Gail Berry. Gail, this is Cindy Halley. And, of course, you know Bob and Betsey." I watched as Bob and Betsey nodded. They had all been a part of Ron's life long before I ever came around...

There was a funny silence for a second. None of us knew quite what to say. Gail was the only one who didn't seem in the least embarrassed. Why would she be? She had deliberately come over and spoiled everything.

Then she put her hands on the table and gazed directly into Ron's troubled-looking eyes. "So, I see you've changed your taste in girls," she purred. "Going for the gangly tomboy type, huh?"

I wanted to die on the spot. Bob and Betsey averted their eyes, embarrassed by Gail's behavior.

"Skip it, Gail," Ron snapped, his annoyance written all over his face.

"What's the matter, big boy?" Gail continued. "Can't stand the truth?"

"Gail, I don't know what your problem is, but get out of here before I do something I'll regret. Just leave me alone. Okay?" He was really angry now.

Before she could respond, a crowd came up to our booth. "Hey, how's it going, Ron?" said one of the boys.

Ron looked relieved. "C'mon over," he said. "I want to introduce you to my new girl. Guys, this is Cindy. Cindy, here're Jim Reade, Steve Bates, Susan Werner, Marcy Johnson and Jamie Sanderson from the Drama Club."

"Nice to meet you," I said, thrilled that Ron had called me his girl. In the next few minutes I listened as they talked about the upcoming play, speculating on who was going to get the leading roles. I wanted to join in the conversation so much I nearly said something about Ron getting the part of Romeo. But remembering my promise, I kept quiet. Sometime during this exchange Gail took the opportunity to leave, and before long I forgot all about the ugly scene.

I wanted the night to last forever, but Ron had to drive me home before my midnight curfew. As he walked me to my door, I felt warm all over. Something told me that he really meant what he said about my being his girl and that this was *definitely* not going to be our last date. We'd just had too much fun. Ron's hand holding mine sent chills up my arm and through my body. The sky was clear and still and sprinkled with stars, as if providing a backdrop for the most perfect night I could remember.

At the door, I fumbled for my key. "Goodnight, Ron," I murmured, suddenly feeling awkward again. "It was...I had...thanks for a great evening."

"No, thank you!" Ron said. He was facing me, smiling, as we stood together on the front steps. I trembled in the cool night air, wondering if he was going to kiss me. I'd read about kissing so often—and I'd seen pictures of people kissing in every single movie I'd seen in the last ten years. So why did I feel as if I wouldn't know how?

Ron must have sensed my worry, because he took my hands gently in his. Then he leaned forward and ever so lightly touched his lips on my nose. It felt so soft and slight—like the touch of a feather.

"Cindy." Ron looked at me one last time before leaving. "It was a nice evening, but a little too crowded." He paused. "I'm really sorry about what Gail said."

Before I could answer he added, "Next time, Cindy, let's make it just you and me. Okay?"

"Okay," I repeated. Smiling, I let myself into the house. His last words echoed in my ear as I floated happily up to my room. *You and me...you and me.*

Chapter Nine

Sunday was a drag. Ever since I had returned from my date with Ron, all I could think about was seeing him again. I knew that probably wouldn't happen until Monday afternoon in study hall. Still, I couldn't help hoping that maybe, just maybe, he'd call and suggest going out for a walk or a ride. Whenever I walked past one of the phones in our house—we had extensions in the kitchen, the den, and in the upstairs bedrooms—I would look at it hard and wish for it to ring.

I'd heard about mental telepathy, and wondered now whether it really worked. I figured there was no harm in trying, so I made an attempt at it. I stared at the telephone and concentrated real hard: "Please, Ron, if you can hear me, please call me right now! Do you hear me, Ron?" But no matter how hard I concentrated on Ron's face, there was no answering phone call. Oh, the phone *did* ring a couple of times, stopping my heart dead, but it always turned out to be Helen or someone for Christine. One guy, I thought, might have been the guy I'd seen with Christine on Friday night. But I put that out of my mind when Helen called for the third time about a math problem that she just couldn't figure out.

"By the way, Helen," I asked her, "have you been hearing funny voices this morning?"

"No," she said, "unless you mean my little brothers and sisters. They're playing Martians."

"No!" I said impatiently. "I mean a little voice in your head telling you to call me."

"I don't think so. Why?"

"Because I've been sending out signals for someone to call me today by mental telepathy."

"Who needs mental telepathy when you can use the phone?"

"I don't dare call Ron!"

"What does Ron have to do with this? I thought you said you were calling *me* by mental telepathy."

"No, silly!" I sighed impatiently. "I was trying to get Ron, but since you keep calling, I thought I got my signals crossed!"

"Listen, Cindy," I heard Helen answer, "stick to algebra, okay? I don't want you messing the whole town up with your mental telepathy stuff. Now, did you get problem number nine on page sixty-seven? These things are driving me crazy!"

"Yeah, I think I've got it."

As I fumbled through the pages, Helen said, "You'll never guess what happened! Jason asked me out for next Friday night!"

"Oh, yeah?" I tried to sound interested, but my mind was stuck on Ron.

Helen went on and on about Jason and eventually I just tuned her out. My brain had made a recording of my date with Ron and the things he had said played over and over in my mind. When it got to the part where Ron brought me home and stood with me on the doorstep, the needle always got stuck, and I would hear my favorite words over and over again: "Next time, Cindy, let's just make it you and me. Okay?"

After Helen hung up, I gave up on the mental telepathy and picked up a copy of *Romeo and Juliet.* I figured that if Ron was going to be Romeo, I'd better catch up on the play. After reading it for a few minutes, I found myself thumbing through the play to find the love scenes. Then a terrible realization hit me: if Ron was going to be Romeo, somebody else would be Juliet. Would she be kissing him at every rehearsal? Suddenly I felt depressed. What if Ron fell in love with her?

As if to emphasize my feelings of gloom, it

started to rain. The sky turned an ominous shade of dark gray, and I had to turn on a light in order to keep reading.

"It's raining cats and dogs!" my father called out from the den.

"When it rains, it pours!" Mom answered from the kitchen. I groaned out loud. My parents *would* have to get corny at a time like this. With this weather, it was a sure thing that Ron wouldn't come over or suggest a ride. Not that I really expected him to. After all, he hadn't mentioned anything last night. But now I couldn't even daydream about it anymore.

"So how was your date?" I looked up to see Christine plop into the chair next to me. Although it was nearly noon, she'd just gotten up and hadn't put on her makeup yet. I decided she looked a little less mean without it.

"Okay," I said.

"Just okay? So what did you do?"

"Oh, nothing special." I wasn't about to confide in her. "We just went to a movie, and then had something to eat at Jack's."

"Well," Christine persisted, getting a bit annoyed. "What movie? Who'd you see at Jack's?" I thought she had a lot of nerve asking me all those questions when she never wanted to tell me anything about *her* dates. Remembering the stranger I had seen just two nights before outside my own window, I wondered what Christine would say if I asked her about *him*. Instead, I just replied, "As a matter of fact, we double-dated. But I don't know if you know them."

"Well, who were they?"

"Bob Falmouth and Betsey White." I couldn't keep myself from bragging. Bob and Betsey were two of the most popular seniors at Northdale.

Christine looked at me scornfully. "What do you mean, I don't know them? *Of course* I do. They're both in the Drama Club, stupid. Anyway, they're seniors, aren't they?"

"So, you don't know everybody that's a senior, do you?"

"Yes, I do."

"Oh, yeah?"

"Yeah! In fact, I know Ron better than you do." Now my sister was treading on dangerous ground, and I resented it.

"Maybe you've known him longer than I have," I told her, "but I know him better."

"How do you know? You can't tell from just one date!"

"Maybe you can't," I said. "But *I* can."

"Oh, come off it, Cindy! One date and you turn into a know-it-all."

"Look who's talking! You act like dating was invented just for *you*!"

"Girls!" Dad called from the den. "What's going on? It's hardly noon, for Pete's sake!"

It was then that I remembered my resolution not to fight with Christine anymore. But as usual, it was too late.

As if on cue, my mother walked into the room. "I have a great idea, girls," she said cheerfully. "Since the weather's so terrible, why don't we go up to the attic and get out our winter things? How about it?" It was her way of calming things down between us.

"Sure, Mom," Christine answered, not very enthusiastically. Her mind seemed to be on other things. I remembered the phone call earlier that morning. She had been asleep when the mystery boy called. He wouldn't leave a message, so nobody had told her about the call. Was she waiting for him to call the way I was waiting for Ron?

Before I could think about it any longer, I got up and followed Mom, who was already halfway up the stairs to the attic. Taking our winter things out of mothballs was a ritual we followed every year when the weather got cold. I loved prowling about in the dusty gloom of the attic. It gave me a chance to look at things I had put away but couldn't bear throwing out—like old dolls or school papers from third grade. I knew that even if I had tried to throw them out, Mom would fish them right out of the garbage again. She could get so sentimental about our childhood mementos. Sometimes we'd be so engrossed in finding old things that we'd never get around to taking out the sweaters as we'd originally planned.

It looked like that would happen today. Within a minute Christine began to rummage around in an old trunk. She pulled out an old, black wool shawl that had belonged to my grandmother. Throwing it over her shoulders, she took a turn around the attic, singing "Romeo, Romeo, wherefore art thou, Romeo!"

"Hey, that's a good idea," I agreed graciously, feeling a little guilty about the fight we'd had earlier. "That shawl would be just super for the play."

"Could I wear it, Mom?" Christine squealed, doing another turn toward the stairs, where she leaned over the railing as if she were on a balcony. "It's just perfect."

Suddenly my blood ran cold. Before my mother could answer, I asked, "What do you mean? They haven't chosen anybody to be Juliet yet. What makes you think it's going to be you?"

Christine smiled secretively while she cuddled the shawl close around her face. "I know it's going to be me."

"How?" I demanded again. I could feel myself turning pale as I realized what this could mean. Still, I didn't want to admit I'd be jealous if my sister played opposite Ron.

"I just know, that's all," Christine stated matter-of-factly. "I know I'm right for the part, and I'm going to get it."

"You're conceited, that's what you are," I snapped. But deep down inside I knew that Christine did have a good chance of getting the part. She was one of the best actresses in school.

"Oh, yeah?" my sister retorted. "I just know

what I'm good at, and what I'm not good at."

"Well, you're pretty lousy at being modest!"

"When you're an actor, you can't afford to be modest."

"Well, how about trying to be a sister, for once?"

"*Look who's talking!* You picked all the fights today!" she screamed at me, flinging the shawl at my feet.

Just then we heard a door close at the bottom of the stairs. It was then that we remembered Mom—she had simply walked out and we hadn't even noticed. Suddenly, feeling very ashamed, Christine and I finished the job of getting the winter things ready. Neither of us exchanged another word for the rest of the afternoon.

The only thing that cheered me up was counting the hours until I'd see Ron again.

Chapter Ten

Every day during the next week, I entered study hall with anticipation, and each time I was sorely disappointed. Ron didn't show up at all! By Friday, when I entered the large, dismal auditorium, I just knew it was hopeless.

He wasn't there again! Taking my seat in the hall, I took out my books, trying to ignore the empty chair in back of me in order to study. I had a geology test next period, and I'd been so shaken by Ron's disappearance that I was barely able to study for it all week.

It wasn't any different now. The words in the book just swam before my eyes: "Continental shift...glacial deposition...volcanic eruption... fault zones..." Finally I closed the book in despair and stared out ahead of me. Who cared about how the earth was formed millions of years ago? All I knew was, the world I was in now, *my* world, was crumbling under my feet. It was Friday, and I hadn't seen or heard from Ron all week. I knew he was in school, because Christine had mentioned seeing him in Drama Club every day. As she had predicted, she was indeed going to be playing Juliet to his Romeo. Yet he hadn't shown up in study hall—or bothered to give me a call.

I felt a sickening wave of fear. Was Ron trying to avoid me? At first I tried to cast the thought out of my mind, but it stuck there. Maybe he'd really had a rotten time last Saturday night. I searched my mind desperately for a reason. Had I said something? Had I *not* said something? Had I done something stupid?

I had been looking forward to seeing him in study hall every day—so we could joke and talk and get to know each other better between dates. Now that he wasn't here, he'd probably forget all about me and never ask me out for Saturday nights again.

Saturday night! I sat up in my chair as if jolted by electricity. At this rate, I wouldn't have a date for tomorrow night. I'd really looked forward to it so much—and now it looked as if it would never happen.

I watched gloomily as a short, blond freshman boy walked up to Miss O'Toole for a bathroom pass. She gave him one, but with a frown, as if she knew he just wanted an opportunity to get out of Study Hall.

Poor Miss O'Toole! She was always suspicious, and never forgot a single misdemeanor committed in her classes. I stared at her for the first time with sympathy. Somehow today she looked a bit different—her normally sharp eyes looked softer than usual, even a little concerned. Could it be that Miss O'Toole developed an affection for those who had suffered at her hands? A scenario developed in my mind. Miss O'Toole had once been a young girl in love with a boy in study hall. Then he left her heartbroken, to pine away forever in this very room, until finally she changed into a bitter, vindictive woman. Now she was doomed to watch over study hall for the rest of her life—to make sure no other young girl fell in love the way she had. It was an interesting thought. If I wasn't so upset about Ron, and if the bell hadn't rung, marking the end of study hall, I might've even made up a short story about it for English class.

"Hey, Cindy!" I turned around to see Carol Astor and Debby Colby trying to catch up with me in the hall. It was between periods and the corridor was packed. I had just barely two minutes to make it to geology, and I wanted to use every last second to look over my notes for the test. I didn't want to stop, but Carol and Debby were the type who'd never forget a slight like that. "Hi, girls," I said.

"What're you doing Saturday night, Cindy?" Carol asked. She and Debby moved through the crowd and were now walking on either side of me. For the life of me I couldn't figure out why they'd want to know. They hardly ever spoke to me.

"Nothing special," I answered. "Why?"

I glanced over at Carol suspiciously. Her hair was brushed and styled meticulously. I knew she spent hours in the girls' bathroom getting it just right. Both she and Debby were always comparing makeup and trying out each other's lipsticks, rouges, and eyeshadow between classes. I sometimes wondered if they weren't using these makeup sessions as a cover-up for eavesdropping on people's private conversations. Even Christine had mentioned earlier this week that she'd been in the girls' room confiding to one of her friends about something Jim Hoog had said, when suddenly there were Carol and Debby trying on mascara.

"Not going out with Ron?" Debby asked.

I whirled around and looked at her. Did she know something I didn't?

"What do you mean?" I tried to act cool but felt panic-stricken.

"Well," Carol began, "maybe you'd better ask your sister, Cindy. I hear they're really taking *Romeo and Juliet* seriously."

Before I could ask her what she meant by that, the bell rang, marking the end of the five-minute break between periods. Debby and Carol ran off for their classes. I thought bitterly about what they had said, and tried to put it out of my mind. Of course it was all rubbish. They were just mean gossips who interfered with everybody's life because they weren't happy with their own.

But one thing puzzled me: why would they make up a story like that and tell it to me? I thought back to the shawl in the attic, to Christine getting the part in *Romeo and Juliet,* and to what she had said about Debby and Carol listening to her conversation in the bathroom. Was it Ron she had been talking about?

I entered the classroom shaking all over and feeling dizzy. My teacher, Mr. Sommitt, began handing out the geology tests. I looked at the paper—and couldn't make out any of the words. The other kids' faces and the desks started spinning, and then everything went black.

I awoke a few minutes later in the first-aid room. When I asked what I was doing there, Mrs. Dean, our kindly old nurse, told me I'd fainted. I lay there looking up at the ceiling in wonder. It was the first time in my life I'd fainted. It was kind of a nice, floating feeling, especially right before I came to. It felt as if I were climbing out of a cloud.

Suddenly I bolted up from the bed. "My geology test," I gasped.

Mrs. Dean felt my forehead and said, "Take it easy. It seems you have a slight case of the flu."

Some flu, I thought. Helen would've called

this an anxiety attack. Although I didn't dare say anything to Mrs. Dean, I knew in my heart that one simple appearance from Ron Peters would make me feel better again. All I said was, "Mrs. Dean, will you please get me a glass of water? I feel thirsty."

"Of course, dear," Mrs. Dean answered. "And don't worry about the exam. You've been excused."

When she left the room, I said out loud, "Thanks for saving me from failing the geology test, Ron." It was a funny thing to say, because inside I really wanted to cry.

Chapter Eleven

On Saturday morning, I called Helen and asked her if she'd go to the mall with me. I needed some more school supplies, but most of all, I needed somebody to talk to.

"Oh, Cin, I'd love to, but I promised Mom I'd help her go food shopping," Helen answered. "With six people in the family, there's a lot of bags to carry. Did I tell you that Mom and I have a trick for making shopping faster? You want to know what we do?"

"What?" I asked indifferently. The last thing I wanted to hear about was food shopping. But since Helen had gone out with Jason last night she was giddy with happiness—and that always made her want to talk about silly things.

"Well," Helen went on, "Mom and I have the

supermarket arrangement memorized. So we both get separate shopping carts..."

Just then I heard my mother talking to Christine in the kitchen. "Christine, dear," she said, "what time did you get back last night?"

"And then Mom starts shopping at the beginning of the store—you know, the bread section..."

"About midnight," Christine answered. Something about her face made me take notice.

Helen's voice droned on. "And then I take the cart with Sally and zoom over across the store..."

My mother looked puzzled. "But Jim called at eleven and asked for you. I thought you'd already come home, but I couldn't find you anywhere. Where were you?"

Christine turned pale, even under the make-up she wore.

"And then Mom and I work our way down the aisles toward each other and meet in the center..."

"Jim wasn't feeling well, so he went home early," Christine said, avoiding my mother's eyes. "And then Fran and Eric and I stayed at Jack's for another soda."

"Ohh. So that explains it," Mom said. "I couldn't figure out where you were, but then I fell asleep. After I heard you come in I was too tired to get up and ask you."

"...lately I've done the entire shopping for the center aisle before Mom ever gets there. Of course, my little brother Billy is a lot more trouble than Sally, so Mom has a harder time..."

"She's lying," I said.

"What do you mean?" Helen sounded incredulous. "Why would Mom lie about a thing like that?"

"Not your mom," I said. "My sister's lying. I could tell from the look on her face while my mother was talking to her. You know what she's up to?"

"Oh, Cindy," Helen interrupted me. "You're crazy! I don't know what in blazes you're talking about. I gotta go. See ya!" I heard a click and then silence.

For a minute, I stood staring at the telephone. Then I grabbed my coat and bag and headed for the door.

"Oh, Cindy," Mom called from the kitchen. "Pick up some bread on your way home, will you? I'd ask Christine, but she's got rehearsal this afternoon."

"Like hell," I muttered, slamming the door behind me. It was obvious to me now that Christine was up to no good. I just hoped desperately it had nothing to do with Ron...

The mall was as crowded as ever. Mayfield's Department Store was so packed that I didn't even bother going in. The line in the ice cream store extended all the way out the door. There was standing room only in the pizza parlor. Everywhere I looked the shops were jammed, and the walkways between the stores were filled with streams of people.

As I walked toward the drug store a kid bumped into me and I nearly tripped. But I didn't care. I didn't feel claustrophobic either, the way Dad always did during Christmas shopping trips to the mall. Today the crowd made me feel safe, as if I belonged somewhere.

Despite the diversion of the crowd, my thoughts kept returning to Ron. Where was he now? I kept coming up with the same depressing conclusion—what does it matter where he is if he's not with me? Chalk it up to experience, I told myself stoically. You're lucky you even had one date with him. At least now nobody can say you're sixteen and never dated.

I felt my eyes start to burn and I blinked back a tear. You just don't have what Gail and Christine have, I told myself. It's not just looks. It's . . . sex appeal. Something I'd never have, ever.

Though my eyes were blurred with tears, I was suddenly aware of someone walking toward me and calling my name. He wore a plaid wool jacket, and his brown hair fell into his eyes. *Ron!* I gasped in disbelief. Yes, it really was Ron. Hurriedly I passed a hand through my hair. I must be a mess! But I had no time to do anything about it. In another second he was standing right in front of me.

"Hey, Cindy, fancy seeing you here!" he said with a grin.

"Hi," I said, overcome with awkwardness.

"Hi," Ron repeated. He looked distracted, as if something was on his mind. "Have you had lunch yet? How about a snack? I have a half hour. I'm on my lunch break, and—"

"Lunch break?" I echoed.

"Yeah, remember I told you my father was manager of Mayfield's?" Ron looked at me questioningly. "So I'm helping out in the stock-room..."

Of course Ron had told me, but I'd forgotten.

"It's been a bit rough, lately, though," Ron went on. He had taken my arm and we were walking past the fountain. "...since rehears-als, I mean. I hardly have any time."

"Oh, I see," I answered. But the despondent look on my face must have made him feel guilty.

"Look, Cindy, I'm sorry," Ron began. His face flushed slightly and I dreaded hearing his next words. Was he going to tell me now that it was a mistake, that there'd be no more dates? That he'd fallen in love with someone else? Like Christine, his Juliet?

"I really wanted to see you in school and talk to you about the weekend, but I've been so tied up..."

"That's okay, Ron," I lied. What else could I say? I turned away so he wouldn't see my face. He was leading me into a sandwich shop now.

"Honest, Cindy." Ron looked distraught. Could he really mean it? Or was he just embarrassed about running into me at the mall and felt he had to say something? "May I help you?" A red-haired boy wearing an apron peered over the counter at us.

"Tuna on rye," Ron answered quickly. He turned to me. "Cindy, would you like a sandwich? I'm sorry I have to rush you, but I don't have much time." He groaned, "Oh, what a drag! If I had known you'd be here."

You could've called me, I thought. But I simply said, "A hotdog please. With mustard."

As we sat down to wait for the sandwiches, Ron took my hand. "Listen to me, Cindy," he said. "I'm sorry I didn't call you. Honest I am. But here's what I'm up against. I have school from eight-thirty to three. Then I work here from three-thirty to six-thirty after school and all day on Saturday. Now that I'm going to be Romeo, I've got rehearsals every Monday, Wednesday, and Thursday evenings. It turns out that's not even enough, so we're meeting Saturday nights as well. Do you know what that means?" He sighed deeply. "I've got only Tuesday and Friday nights free—and I've got to reserve them for homework."

Ron looked almost desperate now, and I began to feel sorry for him. But not as sorry as I felt for myself. All I could think was, *what about me?* When would Ron have time for me?

"What about Sundays..." I began feebly.

"Gee, Cindy!" he answered. "It's the only free day I have left, and I spend it at home. I never see my family otherwise, and..." He hesitated.

"You see, I have a younger sister who's crippled, and on Sundays, I like to spend time with her."

"Your sandwiches." The redheaded kid set a tray before us. "Two Cokes, right?"

"Right," Ron and I said in unison. I felt awful. Here I was worried about looking ugly and having no sex appeal, and Ron had a disabled sister. I toyed with the ice cubes in my Coke uneasily. I'd been so selfish, so wrapped up in myself! "I'm sorry, Ron—"

But he cut me off. "No, *I'm* sorry," he insisted. "Somewhere, somehow, I should've squeezed in a phone call. Especially now that I had to give up study hall."

I looked up. "You what?"

"More practice," he explained. "I know I should have told you sooner. I love acting and I love school, and I love making money, and I love my sister, and I love..." He stopped for a second before going on. "I just don't have time for everything. Understand?"

He looked down at his sandwich, and I saw a faint blush creep up his neck. What—or who—else did he love? Was it Christine? Sitting there watching him, I wanted so badly for him to love me, to be mine. Then I could say "I love you" as much as I wanted to and not be afraid he really loved somebody else.

Ron glanced at the clock overhead. "Darn, got to get back. Want to walk me back to the store?"

"Of course," I said.

We walked back in silence, holding hands. Soon we reached Mayfield's and Ron moved to say goodbye. In a flash, I realized he was going to kiss me. Suddenly there was no time to think twice, to stop, to tell him people were watching. His mouth pressed down on mine and he held me tight. I couldn't pull away—I didn't want to. I couldn't even tell myself I didn't know how to kiss because I felt myself responding automatically to the movement of his lips on mine.

As quickly as it had happened, it was all over. Ron rushed off into the swinging doors of Mayfield's, calling behind him, "I'm late, Cindy! See you soon, okay?"

"See you soon," I echoed happily. I was still smiling from the kiss. I glided blissfully through the mall after that, down every walkway, over every bridge, through all the promenades. I couldn't believe it—*Ron had kissed me! Ron had kissed me!*

Passing a card shop, I spotted a large pink birthday card in the window that read, "Sweet Sixteen and never been kissed." I'm sixteen and I've been kissed, I thought happily.

Impulsively, I walked into the store. There were cards everywhere for brothers, fathers, aunts, uncles, sisters, cousins, nephews, nieces, grandparents. A feeling of affection swept over me as I thought of my family. My parents were the best in the whole world. Even Christine wasn't so bad when I got right down to it.

I bought cards for everyone. "To the greatest Mom in the world..." "The greatest Dad..." "To a super sister." I paid for the cards and put them in my bag. Heading for the bus home, I felt as if I were flying on top of the world.

It wasn't until I got home that I realized I'd forgotten all about the bread.

Chapter Twelve

"Why, thank you, darling," Mom said when she saw the card I had placed on her plate at dinner time. "How sweet of you. What's the occasion?"

Watching as she and Dad opened their envelopes, I felt really silly. The blissful happiness I'd felt after Ron's kiss had worn off a bit. Now getting these cards struck me as a dumb, babyish idea—even downright stupid!

"You know, Cindy," my father beamed, "this reminds me of when you were in grade school and you used to bring home all those cute drawings."

Christine wasn't so impressed. "What are you—some kind of Polyanna?" She wrinkled her nose. "What's with you, anyway?"

"Christine!" Mom looked at her sternly. "Cindy deserves better than that."

"She's right, Christine," Dad agreed.

"All right, all right." Christine gave in. "I'm sorry. It's a nice idea." She frowned and turned her attention to the script she had next to her plate. Some apology, I thought. But I didn't say another word about it.

A few moments later the silence of the dinner table was interrupted by the beep of a car horn.

"It's the kids!" Christine announced, grabbing the script and her jacket and running to the door. "Got to go to practice. Bye." With a swing of her blonde hair, she was out the door.

I couldn't help but wonder who was in the car. Was Ron in it, waiting for Christine? I could still feel his kiss on my lips, and the thought made me tingle all over. Then another, dark thought struck me. Had they gotten to the kissing part yet in *Romeo and Juliet*? Would Ron be kissing Christine tonight the same way he'd kissed me?

"What's the matter, Cin?" Mom looked at me as she got up to clear the table. "Not upset about what Christine said, are you?"

"Oh, no," I answered, a little too quickly. *Not about what she said, but about what she might do.*

My father didn't seem to notice my apprehension. "Now that we've got you here alone," he said, "I think the time is right to talk about your future, Cindy."

"Huh?" I said, puzzled.

Dad took a sip of his coffee and continued. "I realize that you've been a little intimidated lately by Christine's accomplishments," he explained. "But you have to realize that Christine is a bit of an actress, and tends to exaggerate what her real achievements have been..."

I nodded silently, hoping this wasn't going to be another one of Dad's sermons.

"...and you mustn't confuse noise for power," Dad went on. "But you see, your mom and I don't want to stifle Christine. It's only months before she goes off on her own, and we realize she's storing up a reserve of confidence, so to speak—"

"But it doesn't mean we think your goals are any less important than hers," Mom finished.

I looked up in astonishment. Could it be that my parents really understood how I felt about Christine?

"Lately I've been getting the impression you think she's more important than I am," I admitted.

Mom walked over and hugged me. "Oh, Cindy, you silly baby!" she said. For an instant, I did feel like a little child. I wanted some babying from my parents. Then I remembered Ron's kiss and I realized that growing up did have its pleasures, too.

After dessert the three of us went into the den to talk about which colleges I should apply to. After an hour, we'd settled on four schools. I suppose some kids in school—like Carol and Debby—would've thought it was a pretty dull way to spend a Saturday night, but I was happy. I felt as if I was renewing my relationship with my parents. Deep down inside, it felt good.

"And if you like, you could go with Christine to the Talent Agency in Chicago and try a little modeling in the summer or between terms," my mother said toward the end of our talk.

"Who, me?" I pressed my hand to my chest and looked at her in amazement.

"You've grown into a beautiful young woman, Cindy," Dad said. "Don't put yourself down so much. Not that I'm wild about modeling for either of you. But if that's what you wanted to do, I wouldn't stand in your way."

I gulped and drank some more coffee. My parents thought I was pretty enough to model? Amazing!

The sound of the phone ringing interrupted us.

"It's for you," Mom said, holding the phone out to me.

I could tell by the look on her face that it wasn't Helen or one of my other girlfriends. My hand trembled a little as I reached for the receiver. Could it be Ron? What would I say to him in front of my parents?

"Hello?" I said hesitantly.

"Hi, Cindy," said Ron in his deep friendly voice. "I just wanted to ask you something quickly before I go back into rehearsal."

"Sure, Ron, what's up?" I heard myself saying, trying to stay cool. I wished more than anything that my parents would go clear the dishes, or something. But they just sat there, Mother knitting, and my father poring through *Lovejoy's Guide to Colleges*.

"Well, since this weekend's been shot, as far as going anywhere or doing anything," Ron was saying, "I wondered whether you could meet me after school on Tuesday? I have an hour free before I have to go to work. I thought we could go to Jack's for a little snack."

"Sure, Ron, that would be super," I said happily. "Where shall I meet you—at the back entrance, behind the cafeteria?"

"Sure, that's great. About three. Oh, by the way, Christine wants to tell you something."

I felt my stomach tighten. What was Christine doing with him? Then I remembered—rehearsal.

"Okay. You calling from school?"

"Oh, no, school's closed weekends," Ron answered. "We're practicing at my house tonight."

"Your house?" I echoed. A lump started to form in my throat. My own sister was spending Saturday night in Ron's house, while I stayed home alone with my parents! Why hadn't she told me?

"Yeah," Ron answered. "We have a rec room downstairs, so there's plenty of room to practice. And my sister gets a chance to watch, too. Because she's handicapped, she usually always gets left out of everything. This gives her a chance to get together with other kids."

I felt a pang shoot through me. What about me, Ron? I thought. Why didn't you invite me to come and watch? How could you kiss me today and then not want to be with me tonight?

Then Christine got on the phone. "Cindy, listen, tell Mom and Dad I'll be home around 12:30. Rehearsal's running late tonight."

"Sure," I answered.

"Oh, and Ron says goodbye and that he'll see you on Tuesday. Bye."

The telephone went click and then there was silence. My parents stared at me expectantly.

"Good news?" my mother ventured.

"Ye—yeah," I stammered. "Ron asked me to meet him after school on Tuesday. And Christine will be a little late tonight."

My father lifted his reading glasses off his nose disapprovingly. Was he upset about Christine—or about my date?

"I don't think I approve of weekday dates," he began to my consternation. "I realize how much having a new boyfriend means to you, but school work still comes first, especially after the discussion we've just had about colleges. You know I'm depending on you to help me pay your college tuition by studying hard and winning at least a partial scholarship. That's going to mean a lot of extra effort on your part. I'm afraid I must limit your dating to weekends only."

I knew Dad meant well, and normally I would've been only too willing to please him, but the thought of missing out on seeing Ron on Tuesday was suddenly just too much for me to bear.

"But then I'll never see him again!" I cried. Dejected, I ran up the stairs to my room. Losing out on seeing Ron on Tuesday was really terrible. Now that I knew what I was missing, it really hurt. I burst into tears. Moments later a knock on my door roused me from my tears.

"Honey, may I come in?" Mom was standing at the door, looking at me sympathetically. I realized my outburst must really have troubled her and Dad.

"Sure, Mom." Quickly, I ran a tissue across my face.

"What's wrong? What was that phone call all about?"

Mom walked across to where I was sitting. Like a kid, I let myself fall into her arms. Then I told her the whole story. Without saying a word she left, presumably to relay the information to Dad.

Later, with my tears dried and my face washed, I came downstairs to the family room. Dad relented and gave me permission to see Ron on weekdays.

"Dad, you're wonderful," I cried, hugging him close.

I was grateful for my parents' love and understanding, but suddenly I wanted Ron's love even more. The feeling was strong in me, and I couldn't push it away. Was that part of growing up, too?

Chapter Thirteen

"Hey, Cindy, what about this one?" Helen held up a bolt of tan gabardine fabric.

"Naw, too dull," I shot back as I sorted through a row of cottons. On Sunday, I'd gotten the inspiration to make a new dress for my date with Ron. So after school on Monday I dragged Helen with me to the mall to pick out fabric. I had a pattern at home for an easy-to-make dress that I'd felt would look great with the right material.

"How about this one?" Helen asked, pointing to a bright orange silk.

"It'd be great if I were a lot older," I said. Looking at the price tag, I added, "Besides, Mom would kill me."

"I don't know why you're going to all this

trouble," Helen commented, eyeing a row of lower-priced blends. "Aren't you going a bit overboard on this guy? Ease up a bit. Christine doesn't get this crazy every time she sees Jim, does she?"

"No," I admitted, "but they've been going out for months already."

"How are they doing, anyway?"

"Okay, I guess," I said, stiffening a bit. Did Helen know anything about Christine and her mystery boy? "Why do you ask?"

"Just curious." But the way she said it made me wonder if she was hiding anything.

I was just about to see if I could pry some information out of her, when she practically shouted, "I've got it!"

I examined the soft powder blue and white fabric she held up. It was beautiful. "Perfect," I agreed enthusiastically.

I paid for the material quickly and we left. Because Helen and I lived in different parts of Northdale, we each raced for separate buses as soon as we stepped out of the store. All thoughts of Christine left my mind as I concentrated on the more pleasant subject of my meeting with Ron.

I was in the den, immersed in my sewing project, when the phone call came. After the first ring, I picked it up, but Christine beat me to it, as I heard her voice on the upstairs extension.

"Hi, is that you, Christine?" the voice on the

other end asked. "I've got so much to talk to you about."

Although I was pretty bad at placing voices over the phone, I was pretty sure it was Ron. I wasn't too concerned about his calling Christine—I figured he had questions about the play and that he'd ask for me after he was through with her. So, I replaced the receiver in its cradle and went back to the dress.

I had been finishing up when the phone rang, so it was only a few minutes later when I took the completed dress to my room.

Curiously, Christine was still on the phone when I passed her room. But the words I heard through her half-opened door made me stop in my tracks.

"Yes, darling, last night was marvelous..."

What was she talking about? There were no play rehearsals last night. And where did she come off calling Ron "darling"? I knew it was wrong of me to listen, but I had to know more.

Although Christine spoke so softly I couldn't make out most of her words, I did hear things like "falling in love...special to me...I've got to see you no matter what anyone says..." It sickened me.

Christine had done things to spite me before, like the time she told Mom I'd broken her expensive bottle of perfume when I hadn't and the time two years ago when she told Barry Mercury I had a crush on him. But this was the absolute worst. If what I was hearing was true—and I wanted to believe I was wrong—she was deliberately stealing my boyfriend from me!

I wanted to burst into her room and confront her, but I knew it would be useless. All my life I'd been runner-up to my older sister and the last thing I needed was to be told one more time how much better she was than me.

So I went to my room and sulked, my depression worsening when Ron got off the phone without asking for me. Was he about to break up with me—for Christine?

Now I was especially anxious to see him on Tuesday. That afternoon, promptly at 3:00, I arrived at the cafeteria entrance, fresh from the ladies' room where I'd touched up my makeup and checked the fit of my dress. Trying not to look too out of place, I watched as the student body of Northdale filed out through the halls, past the cafeteria, past me, and out the back entrance. As usual, there was plenty of pushing and shoving and yelling now that the end of another grueling school day had come.

I wished I felt as carefree as everyone else. But my nervousness grew as the large hand on the clock over the cafeteria door slowly moved around the dial. Five after three...six after three. My anxiety turned to panic. Where was he? Was he going to stand me up?

At 3:10, out of the corner of my eye, I saw a tall boy approaching. My hopes shot up, then fell back down with a thud. It was Jim Hoog. What did he want?

"Hi," I mumbled as he strode up to me. I never did like him much, and I hoped it didn't show. Ron was the only person I really wanted to see right now.

"I'll bet you're waiting for Ron," Jim said without even bothering to say "hi." He had a strange, flushed look on his face, the way he did right after a rough football game.

I stared at him questioningly. "How did you know?"

Jim reached out and put his hand on my shoulder. My skin crawled where he touched me, but I just stood there looking at him. I knew he was going to tell me something, and suddenly I realized what it was going to be.

"I guess you know about Christine and me," he said. "We're through."

My mouth dropped open, but no sound came out. Christine hadn't told me a thing.

Jim went on, tightening his grip on my shoulder. "Cindy, how could she do this to me?"

"I'm sorry, Jim," I said. "I didn't know."

"That Peters guy—it's all his fault," Jim spat out in disgust. "If he hadn't come along this never would have happened."

My worst fear was confirmed! Ron *was* going out with Christine! I couldn't stand to hear another word. I tore away from Jim's grip and ran off. As I fled, the back entrance, the parking lot, the cars, the kids walking home along the grounds—all melted into a blur. I could hear my inner accusations against myself. How could

I have been so stupid? All those times I'd seen Ron and Christine talking in the hall. The play. Christine rehearsing at Ron's house. It was so obvious! But as usual, I'd been too stupid to catch on.

When I got home, I dried my tears before going inside. I wasn't going to let Mom see me crying. It was one thing to come home crying at age ten, but quite another at sixteen. I had to act grown up, even if it killed me.

I made a firm decision right then. I would go to Ron's house and have it out with him. I wouldn't cry. I'd just make him tell me the truth, and let him know I was mature enough to handle it. Wiping my eyes one last time, I opened the back door of my house and stepped into the warm lighted kitchen, where my mother was baking.

But I couldn't fool her. "Why, honey," she demanded, looking at me with surprise. "What happened? You don't look well at all."

I decided to level with her. "Mom—Christine and Jim Hoog broke up last night. Did you know about it?"

"Well, yes," Mom admitted. "But is that why you're upset? Where is Ron? Weren't you meeting him today?"

"Mom." I tried to remain brave. "I know about it."

Mom's blue eyes looked puzzled. "About what?"

I looked at her squarely. "Christine and her new boyfriend."

Mom put a hand to her mouth in shock for an instant, then released it. "Cindy, what in the world? What new boyfriend?"

I sighed wearily. "I guess she'll tell you later. How could she do this to me?"

"I thought you didn't care for Jim," Mom said. "What does this have to do with you, anyway?"

I started toward the door. "Mom, you don't understand. She—they even tried to pretend it was Gail Berry who..."

Mom grabbed my arm as I opened the back door. "For heaven's sake, Cindy. What are you talking about?"

"Ron. Christine broke up with Jim to go out with Ron!" I opened the back door.

"I don't believe that," Mom said, astonished. "And just where do you think you're going?"

"Mom, I have to talk to him."

"Ron?"

"Yes. I have to hear it from him, just to get it out of my system."

"Cindy, listen to me." Mom held the door closed with one hand. "I don't know what's going on with Ron. But, darling, you can't run all over town after him."

"Oh, Mom!" I was yelling now. "Times have changed since you were dating! I'm not going to stay at home and sit waiting around the phone the way you did with Dad. It's stupid and old-fashioned."

Mom took her hand off the door. Her face was

flushed and I knew I'd hurt her. "Okay, Cindy," she said quietly. "Do what you have to do." She turned away from me, as I slipped out the door into the November dusk.

Minutes later, I was making my way across town to Ron's house. The sky had turned completely black by the time I got to the two-story white clapboard house where he lived with his parents and his brother and sister. Taking cover behind an old, thick maple tree, I stood for a minute in order to collect myself. Should I go up to the front door and ring the bell? What should I say?

I imagined what I would say if his mother answered the door. "Hello, why Mrs. Peters. I'd like to know why your son Ron kissed me on the mall Saturday if he didn't really mean it." But even as I thought it, I knew I'd never have the nerve to say such a thing.

Leaving the shelter of the maple tree, I started toward the house. But now my mother's words started to haunt me. What was I doing, tracking Ron down in his own house? He certainly had a right to do whatever he pleased.

Suddenly I felt stupid. Mom and Dad were wrong the other night when they said I was growing up. I was still only a silly sixteen-year-old girl.

I decided to go home then. But as I turned away, noises from a basement window caught my attention. Was Christine down there rehearsing with Ron and the drama group? Dreading what I might see if I looked in the open window, I told myself not to go near it. But I went ahead anyway.

I crept toward it as quietly as I could. Then I knelt down and peered over the edge of the sill. What I saw made me gasp. Inside were two people in each other's arms, kissing passionately. The boy was tall and gangly, with floppy brown hair—the girl was a slender blonde. Ron and Christine! Numbly I turned away and ran off into the darkness, until I found my way home.

Then I ran upstairs to my room and slammed the door shut. I refused to come down for dinner, telling Mom that I wasn't feeling well. I even refused to come to the phone later on when Helen called.

The truth was, I couldn't bear to see Christine. About Ron I could only feel numb, and hurt. But as for Christine, I'd had it. After years of being jealous of her, of wanting her attention and approval, of wishing I looked and acted like her, I now felt only anger and hatred. Weren't sisters supposed to be loyal friends for life? Wasn't an older sister supposed to help the younger one? And what about sisterly love? Briefly, I thought back to when Christine had done my hair for my first date with Ron. Was it only just a week and a half ago? They must have been involved with each other then! He was obviously the mystery man she'd been seeing on the sly.

Nothing made sense anymore. Nothing except the certainty that Christine and Ron had betrayed me. I buried my head in my pillow in despair. Christine was so beautiful, so popular and so talented—I couldn't even begin to compete with her. Why did she take away the one thing that mattered to me?

Around 10:00 a light tapping on the door startled me. "Cindy." I heard Christine's voice from behind the closed bedroom door. "I've got to talk to you."

I stared at the ceiling in silence. There was no way I could face her.

"Christine, if you don't mind, I've got to get to bed. I have an exam tomorrow, and I'm bushed." I summoned all my strength to get out that lie.

My sister persisted. "What's wrong with you?" She stopped for a second and the silence of my room rang in my ears. "Listen, I wanted to tell you about Jim. We broke up today."

I brought my hands up to my head, blocking her words from my ears. Why was she torturing me? Why didn't she leave me alone now? I didn't want to talk to her ever again. No, never, ever, again.

"Not now, Christine," I called back. "Leave me alone!"

I heard my sister sigh loudly, then walk down

the hall to her room. When she reached her own door I heard it open and close.

I hate you, Christine, I thought to myself. I wish you were dead.

Chapter Fourteen

"Hey, what's with you?" Helen remarked as she plunked down her lunch bag and grabbed the seat I always saved for her during lunch period. "You look just like I feel."

"Wrong," I answered gloomily, not even bothering to look up at her. "You couldn't possibly even come close to feeling the way I do."

"Oh, really?" Helen sounded a little hurt. "So feelings are reserved only for you Emily Dickinson types? You think you're the only one with problems?"

I pretended to be busy wrapping and unwrapping my lunch. Of all people, Helen was usually the one I could pour my heart out to. But nothing we'd shared so far had ever come close to this. As furious as I was with Christine,

115

I couldn't talk about her as a liar and a cheat, not even to Helen. Things had just gotten way out of hand. I remembered a time, not so long ago, when all Helen and I talked about was rock groups, or new clothes, or boys or girls in school that we either liked or we didn't like. How complicated things were getting now!

"Oh, Helen," I sighed. "I don't mean you don't have feelings or anything. But you'll never know what it's like to have an older sister."

Helen lifted the plastic lid off of a Styrofoam container holding her usual lunch—a clump of iceberg lettuce with a few slices of tomatoes. It was a wonder she didn't starve to death eating like that. The truth was, she was always ten pounds overweight no matter what she ate.

"No," she agreed, biting into a pale-green leaf. "But I know what it's like to have a younger sister. And that's bad enough."

I nibbled at my peanut butter and jelly sandwich. "I'd give anything to have a younger sister rather than an older sister!" I mumbled.

"Well, I'd give anything to *be* a younger sister rather than an older sister!" Helen retorted. "Younger sisters have it a lot easier, believe me."

"Oh, yeah?" I protested. "Older sisters get first grabs from the moment they're born. They're their parents' favorites. They get more pictures in the baby books and more presents from grandparents. Then when they're older they get all of the privileges. Why, they get absolute authority over their younger sisters, which means they get bossy and tell them just what to do—"

"What's another word for bossy?" Helen interrupted me. Her iceberg lettuce had already "melted" in her mouth, as she put it, and now she was eyeing the peanut butter and jelly sandwich I'd hardly touched.

"Another word for bossy? Authoritarian!" I said.

"No," Helen said. "Try babysitting."

"Babysitting?"

"Yeah, babysitting. As the oldest sister in a family of four kids, having authority, as you say, means I have to babysit an awful lot. That means missing out on dates and school activities and a lot of other good stuff."

"Well, my sister doesn't have to babysit." I smiled. "And I'm the one in our family who happens to miss out on dates."

"You don't miss out because of Christine! If anything, she brings home boys for you to meet," Helen insisted.

Before I could protest, she went on. "And if you didn't have an older sister, you wouldn't be wearing *that*."

I looked down at my aqua-blue pullover sewn with sparkly gold threads. It was a loan from Christine tha⁺ had eventually turned into a hand-me-down. ' So what? Christine didn't want it anymore. It's a *hand-me-down*. Older sisters don't have to get hand-me-downs."

"Right!" Helen agreed. "And believe me, I

wouldn't mind having an older sister to pass me something extra now and then."

I thought bitterly of what my older sister had taken away. I'd give a million sweaters just to have Ron back again. "What about what they take?"

"Take?" echoed Helen. "From my experience, it's the younger ones who take—and sometimes everything I've got!"

I tried to deny that, but Helen wasn't listening. "Ever since Mom took a part-time job," she said, "I have to pick up Sally every day from nursery school. That cuts out hanging out here after school."

"That's pretty bad, Helen," I agreed half-heartedly. "But at least Sally can't take Jason away from you."

"Take Jason away?" Helen stopped and looked at me. "You haven't even given me a chance to tell you what happened with him."

"He never showed up," I murmured.

"Never showed up?" Helen repeated. "What do you mean? We..." Then looking at my pained face she understood. "Are you talking about Ron?"

"Yes," I said. "Anyway, isn't it all over school by now?"

"Isn't what all over school?"

"About Ron and my sister?"

"Christine and Ron? You mean about their being Romeo and Juliet in the play?"

"In real life, too, Helen." There, I'd said it.

"In real life?" Helen let out a laugh. "Christine and Ron? You're crazy! I mean, now you've really flipped, Cindy."

"Oh, yeah?" I retorted hotly. "It's true! So much for older sisters! You always thought I was so lucky to have Christine. You know what she did to me? She took Ron away from me. They both pretended he was interested in me, but they've been going out behind my back."

Suddenly I was aware of the other students around me. Had they overheard? I glanced around me, but no one was looking our way.

"But why would they?" Helen was looking at me in disbelief.

"I guess they used me as a cover-up to hide the truth from Jim Hoog."

Helen wasn't convinced. "Cindy, that doesn't make sense! Why would Christine want to do something like that? Wouldn't it be easier to just break up with Jim if there were someone else she was interested in?"

I took a sip of milk from my carton. Why was my best friend assuming I was wrong and my sister was right?

"Besides," Helen went on, "I saw Ron yesterday after school and I spoke to him. He said he was on his way to meet you. Are you sure you were waiting in the right place?"

"Positive," I answered, but suddenly I wasn't sure. Had Ron really told Helen he was meeting me? Then I remembered the scene in Ron's basement window. No, that had been as real as

Helen was now, sitting next to me picking at my discarded sandwich.

"Well, how long did you wait?" she asked.

"About ten minutes."

"Only ten minutes!" Helen gasped. "You left after ten minutes?"

It suddenly sounded unreasonable, even to me. "It seemed like an eternity," I mumbled feebly. "I figured Ron had stood me up."

"Stood you up?" Helen was shouting now. "Look, Cindy, you may be my best friend, but you're a *jerk*!" A couple of heads turned in our direction.

"Ron didn't stand you up, dummy," Helen said. "You stood him up."

"What?" I shrieked.

"He was on his way to meet you. He was upset because he knew he was late. But he told me his brother had turned up at school and had to talk to him. He figured you'd understand."

"His brother?" Yes, I remembered now. Ron had mentioned an older brother.

"Yeah, I heard he's dating somebody in school, too. So you thought Ron took off with Christine? Boy, Cindy. You really are paranoid. Maybe you should see a shrink."

Now it was my turn to shout. "Look, Helen. Maybe I didn't wait as long as I should've, but I have proof that Ron and Christine have something going."

"Like what?" Instead of being curious, Helen looked at me doubtfully.

"Don't tell me you'd rather believe my sister than me, your best friend," I said angrily.

Helen wrinkled her brow. "You're the only one arguing, Cindy," she said. "And if Ron wasn't your first boyfriend, I'd believe you. But you haven't been the same since you met him. You've just turned into a bundle of nerves."

"Gee, thanks," I said.

"Wait a minute," Helen protested. "Your story is just too farfetched, especially since only yesterday Ron looked very eager to see you. You must've really disappointed him when you stood him up."

"I didn't stand him up!" I yelled. "Do you know what I saw?" Then I told her how I'd seen him and Christine through the basement window. "You know what they were doing, Helen? Kissing—that's what!"

"What?" Helen grabbed my arm. "That's impossible."

"Helen, I saw them"—I pointed to my eyes—"*with my own eyes.*"

Helen thought for a moment. "Wait a minute!" she said, her face brightening. "What time did you see this?"

"About five, just after dark. Why?"

"Then it wasn't Ron!" Helen exclaimed gleefully.

"Don't do this to me, Helen," I said. "I saw

Ron *with my own eyes.* Don't you understand?"

Just then the bell rang, signalling the end of lunch period. The sound nearly drowned out the rest of Helen's words.

"...because I was at Mayfield's with Jason yesterday," she was saying, "at exactly five P.M. And we saw Ron there *with our own eyes.*"

Chapter Fifteen

Helen's words haunted me all through English class. She claimed to have seen Ron at Mayfield's. She'd been there visiting Jason in the hardware department and they'd both seen him. In fact, she even offered to find Jason and have him verify it. But I begged her not to get him involved.

I pondered, too, what she'd said about Ron not standing me up. She'd said he was on his way to meet me. But if that was true, then who had I seen? I was convinced that the blonde head I'd seen through the window was Christine's—I recognized the barrettes she was wearing. But the other head, the one with the floppy brown hair . . . I was baffled.

"Cindy, will you please summarize the homework assignment for the class?" someone said in the far distance.

Yet Helen *swore* she saw Ron at Mayfield's. Jason Greenberg had even talked to him!

"Cindy Halley! Are you listening? Have you done the homework assignment?"

The sound of my name rang in the stillness of the classroom. Suddenly I was aware of thirty pairs of eyes staring at me from all around the room. The angry eyes of Mrs. Hilton, my English teacher, bore down the hardest.

"Uh...excuse me. Could you repeat that?" I asked sheepishly. But I knew I wouldn't get away with it. Mrs. Hilton had called on me twice already. I could hear the other kids smirking and whispering. What exactly was it that Mrs. Hilton had asked me? Something about a homework assignment?

"Cindy!" Mrs. Hilton stared at me impatiently. "As your English teacher I feel it's my duty to inform you that your daydreaming is detrimental to your classwork."

I hung my head in embarrassment at her words, and prayed for the moment to pass on. But Mrs. Hilton kept talking. I wished I could disappear.

"And personally," she went on, "I feel hurt and annoyed that I've been standing here talking all this time, only to realize you haven't been paying attention. I'm here to teach you to the best of my ability. The least you could do is give me the respect that I deserve."

It was obvious that Mrs. Hilton wanted an apology from me. I glanced at her, redfaced. Her grey hair was cut neatly in short layers around her usually kind round face. She wore a plain blue suit, one I saw her wear at least once a week. I knew she didn't earn very much as a teacher, but she loved English literature and obviously liked teaching others to love it, too. She often spent free time after class helping students—including me—with class assignments. The realization struck that I never really *had* given Mrs. Hilton the attention she deserved. Suddenly I felt ashamed of myself.

"I'm really sorry," I answered. "I'll try not to let it happen again."

From her expression, I knew Mrs. Hilton believed me. She was too smart a teacher to be confused about the sincerity of her students. I looked at her gratefully. Somehow turning sixteen and thinking about Ron had made me lose sight of a lot of other good things.

I thought about Mrs. Hilton after English class as I was walking to study hall. With a pang of regret, I realized I'd been treating everybody the same way I'd treated her. I only thought about what was happening to *me*, while ignoring everybody else.

Like Helen, for instance. It occurred to me that while I insisted that she listen to my endless ramblings about Ron, I turned off when she spoke about Jason. I thought of my parents, and realized that I hadn't asked either of them a single question about themselves since school started three months ago.

And then there was Christine. I was so busy envying her good looks, her good luck, and her boyfriends. I just assumed she was having a better time than I was. But was she? Was it right of me to condemn her actions without giving her a chance to defend herself? It must have been hard for her to break up with Jim Hoog. But I didn't know how she felt about it because I was feeling too sorry for myself to care about her or anyone else... except Ron.

I had taken my seat in study hall now, and I thought of the empty seat behind me with a sigh. Had Ron ever been a real person to me? Or was he just a reflection of what I wanted a boyfriend to be?

"Hi, there." A whisper in my ear nearly made me jump with surprise. I turned around in my seat and looked behind me, whirling back just as quickly as I felt Miss O'Toole looking in my direction. She gave me a warning look, but she said nothing. I sighed deeply, not so much out of relief, but because I'd lost my breath. Ron was back! I'd seen the floppy long brown hair and... nothing much else. Yet, I was sure it was him!

Nevertheless I felt totally confused. Here was Ron, sitting behind me again at last—and I didn't know whether to hate him or to love him.

Miss O'Toole had become absorbed in some

test papers. Still, I sat stiffly in my seat, staring ahead of me. I felt totally paralyzed. One half of me wanted to jump out of my seat and into Ron's arms behind me. The other half wanted to run away and never see him again.

"What's the matter—won't you even say hello?" Ron's voice pleaded softly.

My hair was pulled back into a barrette on the right side, and I could feel the soft skin behind my ear tingling from his breath. But still, I couldn't respond. I pretended to be watching Miss O'Toole, but she wasn't even looking up from her desk.

"I'm sorry I missed you yesterday," Ron continued. "Gee, Cindy, you don't give a guy an extra minute, do you?"

I felt my heart racing inside of me. Uncontrollably, my mind focused on that image of Ron kissing Christine.

I turned in my seat, nearly facing him squarely. "How stupid do you think I am?" I accused him.

"What are you talking about?" Ron asked, raising his voice.

"You know very well what I'm talking about," I said. "I saw you and Christine yesterday. I know the score now."

"Cindy," Ron shouted, "you're—"

"Cindy Halley and Ron Peters!" A shrill voice from the front of the hall interrupted us. "Report back here after school."

I twisted back in my seat, but too late. I

looked up at the angry face of Miss O'Toole. "You know I will not tolerate this kind of behavior in my room..."

Looking down, I tried to concentrate on my homework, trying to forget the person behind me. My geology make-up test was scheduled for today and I really wanted to do well on it. But I might as well have turned around and stared at Ron for all I could accomplish. His image was on the face of my textbook and my notes. I closed my book in disgust. Everywhere I looked there was Ron, Ron, Ron. It was no use pretending I never wanted to see him again. I was still madly in love with him—no matter how much of me still hurt.

Mercifully the bell finally rang, releasing me from the torture of being near him. But before I left the auditorium Ron slipped me a note. It read: *Cindy, darling, I don't know what crazy thoughts are running through your head. I've got to talk to you.*

Love,
Ron

Chapter Sixteen

When school let out later that afternoon, I slipped into the girls' room before reporting to detention. With a shaking hand, I took out Ron's note and read it again. I prayed silently that I hadn't totally blown it with him. Maybe, just maybe, there was a reasonable explanation for what I'd seen the day before. Maybe it was just some horrible misunderstanding.

I peered at my reflection in the large mirror hanging over the sinks. Usually, there was never an inch of space in here—there were so many girls pushing and shoving and trying to put on makeup all at once. Now, I had the whole place to myself. I looked alone and pale, standing in front of that big mirror all by myself. Reaching into my bag I pulled out a small compact containing a blusher. Hastily I rubbed some of the pink powder on my cheeks, and then applied some tinted lipgloss to my mouth. It was so important that I looked my best for Ron when I saw him.

The swinging doors pushed open and someone walked in. Looking down, I pretended to fumble through my bag. It just might be Carol Astor or Debby Colby, and I didn't want them to know what I was doing.

"Oh...Cindy!" I heard a familiar voice call. "What're you doing here?" It was Christine!

I looked up at my sister in bewilderment, not knowing what to say. What was *she* doing here?

"Oh, don't tell me." Christine smiled at me, but I could detect no malice in her gaze. "You got another detention!" Her pretty blonde hair fell in smooth, rippling waves over her shoulders. The irritated look she had had lately was gone, and her eyes glowed with happiness. She had the kind of look I'd heard people had when they were in love.

I felt overwhelmed with defeat. I would never be able to compete with Christine. "Yeah," I admitted to my sister. "Miss O'Toole caught me again. I guess Ron told you?"

Christine looked at me with a puzzled expression. "Ron?" she said. "No, I haven't seen him. We cancelled rehearsals today, you know. But, Cindy," she said after a second's hesitation. "I'm glad I caught you. There's someone waiting outside I want you to meet, as soon as I wash this ink off my hands. My pen broke in eighth period, and I've got ink all over me..."

As she washed the blue blotches off her hands hastily, I stood there, feeling completely confused. What was she talking about?

"C'mon, Cindy." Christine tugged at my sleeve. "Bob's waiting, and he's got to get back to work..."

Who is Bob? I wondered. I followed her through the green swinging doors of the ladies' room and out into the hall, straight to a tall young man who stood waiting across the corridor. He was leaning against the wall, smiling in a way I knew very well already, a shock of floppy brown hair hanging over one eye. He looked just like...yet he wasn't! This boy looked much older. In fact, he looked the way I imagined Ron would look when he became a man.

Christine blushed slightly as we walked up to him and she introduced us. "Bob, this is my sister, Cindy." I noticed she had omitted the word "little." "Cindy, this is Bob. Ron's brother."

"Bob Peters," the man repeated, holding out a large, firm hand for me to shake. Suddenly all the pieces of the puzzle came together. What a fool I'd been!

As if reading my thoughts, Bob said, "So this is the young lady my brother's so crazy about?" He grinned, showing white teeth much like Ron's. "Well, I can't say I blame him, knowing how things run in the family!"

At this he put his arm around Christine. She smiled up at him happily, in a way I'd never seen her do with Jim Hoog. Suddenly I realized that Christine had tried to tell me about Jim and Bob last night, but I wouldn't listen. If I had, I wouldn't have gone through all this needless pain! I thought back to the kissing scene in the basement window and suddenly all my grief and anger melted like icicles in a spring thaw. All I'd seen was Christine kissing her new boyfriend! Remembering, I felt a little sheepish—and very stupid.

"Well, it was sure nice meeting you," Bob said, smiling at me and giving Christine a hug. "But my lunch break is over, and I have to head back, I'll be seeing a lot more of you, I'm sure!"

"Lunch break?" I questioned him. "Isn't it after three already?"

"I guess it is!" Bob laughed, looking at his watch. "Just because of your sister, here"—he winked at Christine—"I starve all morning just so I can drive over at three and see her after school. And what do I get for thanks? A dried-out hamburger in the Northdale High cafeteria. I'll bet that burger was left over from when I went to high school—five years ago!"

"Five years ago!" I said. "That makes you—"

"Nearly twenty-three years old," Bob finished for me. "I never thought I'd see the day when some kid like you would look at me like I was an old man!"

"Oh, you're not old," I lied. But I couldn't fool Bob.

"You stick with Ron," he teased. "He's more your age. Let your sister here deal with older men." With that he left.

"He works at Mayfield's," Christine explained. "Training to be manager, so he can take over for his father... Oh, Cindy," she said, looking at me hesitantly. "I wanted to tell you about Bob last night, but you were tired..."

"I know."

"And..." She looked shy for the first time. "Mom told me what you thought about me and Ron. I guess it was partly my fault. I'm sorry I've been acting so secretive around you lately. It's just that I felt so guilty about Bob—you know, not wanting Mom and Dad to know about him..."

"Because he's older?" I ventured.

"Yes." She sighed deeply. "Bob's finally coming over tonight to meet them. I had to tell them about him. I couldn't stand sneaking behind their backs anymore. But I'm positive they'll love him once they meet him."

I smiled at her. "I'm sure they will, too." I was too ashamed to add that, until now, how *she* felt had never even crossed my mind. All I'd been thinking about was how she made *me* feel and what I believed she was doing to me. I'd been so foolish. Had I really believed my own sister would be cruel enough to steal away my very first boyfriend?

The large-faced clock in the hall caught my attention. It was 3:15 and I was late for my detention! Miss O'Toole was going to kill me!

I hastily said goodbye to Christine, adding, "We'll talk tonight, okay?" Then I was off to...who knows what? Things were happening so fast now, I didn't know what to expect. All I knew was Ron would be there, and I had to make things between us better again.

Miss O'Toole was waiting for me when I got to study hall. "You're five minutes late," she pointed out.

"I—I'm very sorry, Miss O'Toole," I said. "What's the assignment today?"

I looked over at Ron, a few rows across from me. He was writing so intently that he didn't even look up to wave "hello." Or was he angry with me? He had every right to be, I thought sadly.

"The assignment today," said Miss O'Toole, "is to correlate some aspect of your life with an academic topic of your choosing—preferably something you're studying this term."

"Whew!" I said. "That's hard. How long should it be?"

"As long as you like. But write quickly. I'm sure we'd all like to get out of here as soon as possible." Surprisingly, Miss O'Toole smiled and returned to her desk.

Thirty minutes later, I glanced up to find Ron staring at me from his desk several rows away. He smiled when he saw me looking. Compared to his older brother, he suddenly looked very young, almost boyish. All at once it didn't matter to me that Ron was captain of the basketball team or the star of *Romeo and Juliet*. Now he was just Ron—somebody's little brother, in the same way that I had always been somebody's little sister.

"When you are finished with your essays," Miss O'Toole called from her desk, "please exchange papers and correct them. I'm busy here with a pile of exams."

I looked up at her. She was certainly full of surprises today. My essay was actually kind of personal, and I wasn't sure I wanted Ron to read it. In about 300 words, I had compared the ups and downs of life to a geological terrain.

Reluctantly I handed my booklet to Ron. He was grinning. Had he and Miss O'Toole arranged this together before I arrived? I watched him go back to his desk, his long legs maneuvering through the aisles. Then my eyes fell to his essay. The title was, *Romeo and Juliet and My Relationship with Cindy Halley.* The words jumped out at me. Did Ron really consider us a relationship?

With my heart beating, I read through the pages of his examination booklet. Not since *Jane Eyre* or *Rebecca* had I ever been so engrossed in a single piece of prose.

Somehow, Ron had contrived to write an entire essay comparing the tragic end of *Romeo and Juliet* to our misunderstanding after school yesterday. He ended it with, "But since you and I are still alive, Cindy, how about a date at Jack's tonight? I know Juliet would have loved hamburgers if they'd been invented in time!"

I almost laughed out loud with happiness at this last part. I glanced over at Ron, who was absorbed in my essay. Compared to Ron's, mine must've been awfully corny and boring—I had somehow managed to compare my recent moods to the formation of a volcano, with the lava as tears. For a moment, I felt embarrassed, but then I decided I didn't care. I looked again at the neat handwriting in front of me. In the school play, Christine was Juliet, but in this essay there was no doubt that Juliet was *me*!

Closing the examination booklet with a grin, I waited for Ron to finish my essay. Then I had a better idea. I uncapped my red felt-tip pen and wrote "Excellent!" in huge red letters on the booklet under Ron's name.

Chapter Seventeen

A month later, on the first day of Christmas vacation, Bob and Christine and Ron and I piled into Ron's car and drove over to Chicago to see the director of Talent Model Agency. Christine had decided not to wait until the summer.

"After all," she said from the back seat, where she was sitting with Bob, "I'll have lots of free time before then—and semester break, and Easter vacation. Maybe they'll need me."

"Correction," Bob said teasingly. "At a hundred dollars an hour, maybe you'll need them."

"Okay, okay," Christine agreed, giggling. "I need them!"

I laughed, adding, "I need a day in the big city. It'll be fun going sightseeing and shopping at all those big department stores. And I want to see Lake Michigan."

Two months ago, I would've been insanely jealous of Christine, going off to a modeling agency. But, now, I realized she wasn't trying to compete with me—she just wanted to give modeling an honest try. And why not? Wouldn't I, if I were in her place?

"Brrrr." Ron pretended to be cold as he turned around a bend in the road and put his arm around me. "Why in the world do you want to see Lake Michigan? They don't call Chicago 'the Windy City' for nothing."

"I won't be cold if you offer me your coat," I teased.

"Hey, wait a minute," Ron protested. "Us big strong men get cold, too." He tightened his arm and I snuggled up against him, watching the highway signs whiz by. I could smell Ron's aftershave—he was wearing my favorite scent—and it made him smell wonderful. Impulsively I reached up and kissed him, totally oblivious to the people behind me.

"Hey, you two," Bob pretended to growl. "Cut that out and mind the road. I'm responsible for you kids."

"Okay, Daddy," Christine and I answered in unison. Then we all burst out laughing. What a strange turn of events we had seen in the past few weeks!

"Isn't it funny, Bob?" Christine remarked. "A

month ago, I felt I wasn't supposed to be with you because you're older, and today Dad let us go to Chicago because you *are* older." Obviously my sister and I thought alike because that was exactly what was on my mind. My parents hadn't been thrilled when Christine had told them, but they agreed that they much preferred having things out in the open. And it wasn't long before they developed a real affection for him. How could they not? He was so much like Ron.

"Yeah, it's funny how things turn out," Bob said. "When your parents first found out about me, they must've felt the way I did when I heard my brother was going to be Romeo and end up kissing my girl every night."

I winced, remembering how I had felt. How painful it had been, believing my sister and Ron were in love!

"You must be relieved it's all over," I said. The play had been a big success, selling out every seat in the house, two nights in a row. Ron and Christine had certainly put a lot of time and energy into it.

"You bet!" Ron said. "Now I'll have some time for fun!" We smiled at each other.

"The best thing will be returning to school after New Year's with a clean slate," Christine sighed. Since her break-up with Jim Hoog, he had bad-mouthed her all over school. In the weeks before Christmas, everyone seemed to be talking about her. It hadn't been a pleasant time for any of us, but it had brought Christine and me a lot closer.

Strangely enough, the whole episode had brought me closer to Helen, too. I thought of my best friend with a smile. She had a new boyfriend now—Doug Fletcher, one of Ron's close friends. She and Jason had "broken up"—if you can call it that—the afternoon they had seen Ron at Mayfield's, the same day I thought I saw him kissing Christine. Helen had tried to tell me about it that day in the lunchroom, but I wouldn't give her a chance. I let out a laugh. Boy, had I been wrapped up in my own problems back then!

An hour or so later we arrived in Chicago. We left Bob and Ron in a nearby coffee shop, because Christine wanted to go to the agency with only me along for moral support. As we made our way up the street a strong wind blowing in from the lake all but destroyed the results of Christine's careful efforts that morning with her hair and makeup.

"I'm a mess!" she wailed, pulling her wool hat closer around her face.

"Don't worry," I assured her, as she tried to smooth down her hair. "Those agency people are experienced. They can tell natural beauty when they see it."

"Natural beauty," Christine scoffed good naturedly. "Judging from the way I look in the morning, I have no natural beauty. Mine comes from pots and jars—and lots of them, too!"

I looked at my sister in surprise. Could she mean that? Surely she was certain of her own good looks! I'd been admiring them for as long as I could remember.

We soon found the building we were looking for and took an elevator to the 20th floor. A sign on one of the doors there said "Talent Models, Inc.," and we went in.

Christine took a comb from her bag and pulled it through her wind-blown hair. A tall, dark woman came into the reception room.

"May I help you?" she asked pleasantly.

"Yes," Christine answered, trying her best to sound poised. "Aren't you Ms. Newson? I'm Christine Halley. We met a few months ago at Northdale High and you suggested that I come up and see you about modeling."

"Oh, yes," Ms. Newson answered, although it was obvious she didn't recognize Christine. "Won't you come this way?"

Christine motioned for me to follow her, and we were shown into a smaller room within the agency. The walls of the tiny office were adorned with color pictures of smiling young women, one more beautiful than the next.

Ms. Newson pointed to two chairs and asked us to sit down. "Now," she said. "Did you bring any photographs?" Christine pulled out an envelope of snapshots from her pocketbook. Dad had taken some of the photographs, while Bob had taken others.

"How about you?" Ms. Newson looked at me.

I felt a blush creeping up my throat. "Oh, no, I'm just here with—" I began, but Christine interrupted me.

"Here are some shots of Cindy," she said, pushing another pile of photos toward Ms. Newson. I started in my seat. Christine hadn't told me she was doing this! Some of the old doubts reentered my mind. What was she trying to do, embarrass me?

Ms. Newson looked at the photographs carefully before returning them to their envelopes. Then she asked Christine, "How tall are you?"

"Five foot six," Christine answered.

"I was afraid so," the woman replied, shaking her head. "You have the perfect face—great bone structure, good eyes, thick hair and a clear, blonde complexion. But, I'm sorry to say, you don't quite fill the height requirement for high fashion modeling. Do you expect to grow anymore?"

"I'm seventeen and a half, so I doubt if I'll get any taller," Christine said.

"So am I," said Ms. Newson. "Have you considered acting, or TV commercials, Christine? You might try there."

"Yes," my sister admitted. "I've already been accepted by a drama school."

"Then go," the woman suggested. "Get your education first, and go on from there."

She turned to me. "How tall are you, Cindy?"

"Five foot nine," I answered, a bit confused. How could Christine have been turned down for her height? I'd always envied it, feeling tall and awkward around her.

"Well, that's good," Ms. Newson said enthusiastically. "How old are you?"

"Sixteen."

"Sixteen." She recorded the information on a white card she had just taken from a file cabinet.

"Have you ever modeled?" she asked.

"Um—uh—no," I stammered.

"Let me give you some advice, Cindy," she said, looking directly at me. "You have all the requirements for a top flight model. But you need a little more poise, some experience under your belt. Where did you say you lived?"

"Northdale," I said, stunned by her remarks.

"Hmm, I believe Mayfield's out there runs several fashion shows a year. Why not try it out? Do some modeling for them. And come back and see me next summer. I may be able to help you out then."

I stared at her dumbfounded. Me—a model? I couldn't believe it!

Ms. Newson reached in her desk drawer, took out a small business card and handed it to me. It read, "Talent Models, Inc." and included an address and phone number. Then she stood up. "Give me a call when school lets out. Meanwhile, good luck to both of you."

After guiding us back to the reception area, she was gone.

"Gee, Christine," I began after we stepped out into the hall and pressed the elevator button. "I'm sorry. It's so silly, to turn someone down over a mere inch . . ." I didn't know what to say. Who would've thought Christine would get turned down for modeling and I would get accepted? It was so crazy, I still couldn't really believe it.

"Oh, forget it, Cin," Christine smiled at me. "I always suspected I was a little short. But what can you do about accidents of birth? I guess you just have to live with them, that's all."

I looked at my sister. She certainly had a healthier attitude toward life than I did.

"Besides," Christine continued, "now that I got *that* out of the way"—she motioned at the door behind us—"I can go full steam into acting. Modeling would just have been another digression."

My sister stuck a finger into the front of my jacket. "But *you*—you could have a whole new career in front of you!"

"Maybe," I answered truthfully. "At the very least it could be a great way to earn some money for college." I was still trying to absorb the news. I couldn't wait to tell Ron!

The elevator doors opened and I pushed my sister in playfully. She nearly hit a tall redhead who stood in the back of the elevator, smiling brightly. Probably one of the models at Talent,

Inc., I thought. But then I looked again. The back of the elevator was mirrored, and there was nobody else there. The tall redhead was me!

"What's the matter, Cin?" my sister asked me. "You look surprised."

"I think I've just had a vision," I said slowly.

"A vision of what?"

"—A vision of the guys stuffing themselves with hamburgers. Come on—let's go before they eat themselves sick!"

"It's nothing," he said, then contradicted himself with a rueful smile. "No, it *is* something, Millie. I have not an unduly high opinion of myself, I trust, but I do have my share of pride. And just now my pride is smarting a bit to think that I should be the cause of your injuring yourself in any way."

"Injuring myself?" said Camilla, regarding him with astonishment. "Whatever do you mean, Larry? How would you be the cause of my injuring myself?"

Larry colored but looked defiant. "Your aunt," he said. "You have expectations from her, do you not? I know several people mentioned the fact to me, and I can see that it might be inconvenient for you to offend her."

Camilla raised her chin. "Yes, but I don't care for that if you don't, Larry. Of course if you are set on marrying an heiress—"

"No, I am set on marrying *you*, Millie. And I am willing to take you in your shift if necessary." There was a glint of laughter in Larry's eyes as he looked down at Camilla. "But still you must see I should hate to be a cause of injury to you, even if it were merely a financial injury. And I am willing to do anything, short of abjuring you altogether, which would help your cause."

"Well, I don't think you need bother about that, Larry," said Camilla. "It happens that Aunt Dorothy has already settled some money on me, and that will be mine regardless of whom I marry—or even if I choose not to marry at all. As for the rest of her fortune, she may dispose of that how she likes. There is no guarantee it would have come to me anyway, and I, for one, shan't worry my head about it."

"Then neither shall I," said Larry. "Have I not already something more valuable than all the fortunes in the world?" He bent to kiss Camilla again.

This interlude might have continued for some time had not the lovers been interrupted by a wheezy voice out of the darkness. "Begging you pardon, sir. Begging your pardon, ma'am. Don't you mind me, no more'n if I was a leaf on that tree over there. I'm just come to fetch Miz Maynard home from the rooms, and I'll be out of your way quick as the cat can lick her ear."

Camilla, turning around with consternation, found herself confronted by a small, bandy-legged man. There was a grin on the man's face, and in one hand he held a lantern, which he shone deliberately into Camilla's and Larry's faces. His grin broadened. "Ah, 'tis Miz Leslie, isn't it? And Captain Westmoreland, 'pon my soul! A very good evening to you both, I'm sure." Still grinning, the man sketched a bow, then set off toward the Assembly Rooms.

"Larry," said Camilla in a weak voice, "do you know who that was?"

"No, but I know I'd like to kick him for his impudence," said Larry, scowling after the bandy-legged man. "Who was it?"

"That was Miss Maynard's manservant. And he is a terrible gossip—a worse gossip even than she is, if you can credit it. By tomorrow, we may expect the whole village to know how he found us this evening!"

Larry laughed. "I have no objection to that," he said. "As far as I'm concerned, the sooner everyone knows we're together again the better. All the same, it does go against the grain to have our hand forced by a fellow like that." Larry shot a calculating look toward the small man's receding figure. "Perhaps we can outmaneuver him. If we were to go back to the ball, for instance, and let it be generally known among our friends that we have come to an understanding, that ought to very effectually spike his guns. What do you think, Millie?"

"Certainly, Larry," said Camilla, tucking her hand in his. "That ought to be as effective as anything." She gave him a rueful smile. "Though what everyone will think, knowing that I arrived tonight with one gentleman and ended up engaging myself to another, I can't think! But I suppose Sir Eustace has already left by now. He meant to take Agnes home, I know."

Camilla spoke these last words in a pensive voice. Larry looked down at her quizzically. "What are you thinking of?" he said. "You're not regretting that you let a baronet slip through your fingers, I hope?"

Camilla laughed. "No, I am thinking that Agnes and Sir Eustace might suit very well if there was some way of bringing them together. He was quite taken with her, I thought—and she certainly appeared taken with him. Would Aunt Dorothy invite her to London for a visit? I wonder. That would probably do the trick."

"I suppose it might," said Larry. "But I must say frankly that I cannot concern myself too deeply in the affairs of other people this evening. My own are too absorbing." He bent to kiss Camilla again.

"Yes," said Camilla, smiling up at him. "Bringing together Stacy and Agnes can safely be left for the future. For now, we must get back to the party."

As she took Larry's arm, she gave him a sparkling look. "Indeed, the other girls will be quite cross with me for monopolizing your attention this evening, Larry. You are one of the guests of honor, after all. And everyone has worked very hard to make this ball successful. You shall have to make it a point to dance with as many girls as possible and to admire all the decorations most assiduously."

"I will if you want me to," said Larry without any very noticeable enthusiasm. "But I tell you plainly that it will be dry work, Millie. I would much rather be out here kissing you."

Camilla laughed. "And that reminds me," she said. "You must remember to patronize the refreshment table, too, Larry. There are some biscuits I particularly want you to try. . . ."

HUSSAR'S KISSES

What Camilla and her friends call sweet biscuits would, of course, be known as cookies in America. Recipes for this type of cookie have been around for centuries, going under a variety of names including Puits d'amour, Love's Wells, and the name given here. Nowadays they are commonly called Jam Thumbprints. This is an authentic recipe in that it contains no leavening, although it will be necessary for American readers to compromise by using almond extract instead of the historically accurate (but legally proscribed) bitter almonds. Be sure to use real butter, as it is essential both to the taste and texture of the finished cookie.

1 1/4 C (10 tbsp.) unsalted butter, softened
1/2 C sugar
1 1/2 C flour
dash of salt
1/2 tsp almond extract
1 egg, separated
1 C almonds, blanched, peeled, and finely chopped
1/2 C jam or jelly

Preheat oven to 375 degrees. In a medium mixing bowl, beat butter and sugar until creamy. Add egg yolk and beat well. Add flour, salt, and almond extract and mix until ingredients are just blended. (If dough is very dry, you may add a tablespoon or two of milk.) In a separate small bowl, beat egg white lightly.

Roll dough in small (one inch) balls. Dip balls in egg white and roll in chopped almonds. Place the balls on a greased baking sheet. Make a hollow in each ball, using your thumb or the handle of a wooden spoon. Dipping the spoon handle in a little flour will keep the dough from sticking.

Bake until lightly browned, about eight to twelve minutes. Fill the hollows of the cookies with jam or jelly as desired. Makes about two dozen.

Put a Little Romance in Your Life With
Fern Michaels

__Dear Emily	0-8217-5676-1	$6.99US/$8.50CAN
__Sara's Song	0-8217-5856-X	$6.99US/$8.50CAN
__Wish List	0-8217-5228-6	$6.99US/$7.99CAN
__Vegas Rich	0-8217-5594-3	$6.99US/$8.50CAN
__Vegas Heat	0-8217-5758-X	$6.99US/$8.50CAN
__Vegas Sunrise	1-55817-5983-3	$6.99US/$8.50CAN
__Whitefire	0-8217-5638-9	$6.99US/$8.50CAN

More Zebra Regency Romances

Put a Little Romance in Your Life With
Rosanne Bittner